Last Stand Of Buckshot Roberts

Last Stand Of Buckshot Roberts

Doug Hensley

Ingram spark

CONTENTS

1 1

CHAPTER THREE

The next day brought more of the same for Hugh Jack. Driving. Scheming. Planning. Thinking of ways to make money. Plotting how to involve himself in his wife's law firm. He drove to his favorite breakfast bar and had the usual. He slowly drove by the law office to see if her car was there. It was. He made his way toward the golf course. He still couldn't get Nickie off his mind.

As he approached the barn, he almost slid off of the entrance road into the ditch. The ruts that Clarice's car had made were still there. He looked to his right and noticed several large pines uprooted on the number ten fairway at the Golf Course. His granite marker honoring his albatross on number ten still stood. The great golf shot he made in the late seventies that produced the marker made Hugh Jack a minor celebrity at the club.

He purchased the property adjacent to the course from Bubba Stewart before the investigation and before he "lost" everything. He had often thought of selling, but the barn came with the well-appointed apartment that now housed

Nickie, and if ever needed, his future home if things didn't work out with number four.

He heard the dogs bark as he approached the barn's front door. They had been inside, dry from the unending rain, unable to run freely for almost two weeks. It had been his habit to take them out one by one and let them run inside the barn while he filled water bowls and fed the horses. He opened the gate to Rip's pen and Rip ran past Hugh Jack quickly covering ground within the barn, expending his stored energy.

The sound of rain beat on top of the tin roof. The daily barrage of thunderous rain and golf ball-sized hail made it difficult for the dogs to sleep. They jumped spastically as he neared each of their pens. Each jockeying for attention. Hoping to be picked, to be released from their prison. It had been too long since they had run freely outside. They were getting fat and out of shape. He worried with Quail season right around the corner, they wouldn't be ready.

As he broke a bale of hay and began dividing it between his two mares, he noticed water puddling near the back door. He opened it and let out a sigh of relief to see the earth holding, the lake was intact. Distracted with the level of the lake, Hugh Jack missed Rip as he ran past him and out into the rain and immediately onto the number ten fairway.

"Rip, come here boy!"

Rip stretched his long legs and ran along the fairway as fast as the standing water would allow. This was the first time in the weeks since the deluge started that he had been out of the barn, and he was making the most of it. He almost looked as though he had a smile on his face as he splashed through the standing water. The other dogs barked excitedly as if cheering on his escape.

"Here boy!" Hugh Jack screamed, trying to raise his voice above the driving rain.

Rip ran back and forth, his paws digging, looking for ground and traction to increase his speed with every gallop.

"Rip, come here dammit!"

His last call turned Rip, and he sped back toward the barn. Hugh Jack called and clapped his hands, trying to maintain Rip's interest. Just as he hit the number ten green, Rip fell out of sight.

"Rip!" Hugh Jack called, his anger increasing with every call. "Rip!"

Although he couldn't see him any longer, Hugh Jack heard Rip whining and barking as if in distress.

"Shit!" Hugh Jack screamed as he slipped his shoes off and slipped his feet in rubber boots. "Son-of-a bitch is running through the woods ... dammit!"

Already wet from sweat, Hugh Jack trudged into the blowing rain pelting his face as he walked into the wind.

As he neared the green, he noticed the back portion looked muddy. He finally made it to the center of the green and saw Rip stuck in mud. The back side of the green had collapsed, making it impossible to walk to Rip.

He eased his body prone onto the green and lay in standing water. He stretched his body and extended his arms as far as he could; his body teetering much like a seesaw, tipping on his midsection. He barely wrapped the tips of his fingers around Rip's collar. Soon he got a full hold and began pulling. The clay created a suction on Rip refusing to release him. After three hard pulls, Rip rose from the depths of the muddy grave. Slowly he continued coming up through the mud until he was completely free. Exhausted, the two of them lay there still, not moving an inch.

Hugh Jack kept a tight grasp on Rip's collar not allowing him to break free and run again. He finally stood to his feet, reached his free hand down into the water, and washed it. He splashed Rip and wiped as much mud from him as he could.

With no lead, he picked Rip up. He stretched his body and stood for a moment before moving. He looked back into the hole from which he had just pulled Rip and the hand of a skeleton looked as though it were reaching out of the mud for him. He stared, fixing his eyes, and squinting through the rain. The mud below the arm fell away, exposing more of the upper arm. The rain kept beating down on the corpse, and as Hugh Jack continued staring, a rib cage slowly emerged through the mud. Earth gave way and broke loose as its foundation slowly eroded from the constant rainfall. The skull broke free and turned twice, rolling just under the exposed portion of the rib cage. The green gave way under the rainfall. Mud and grass continued sliding, now starting to cover parts of the skeleton previously exposed. Hugh Jack trudged his way back toward the barn cradling Rip in his arms.

CHAPTER FOUR

T he alarm clock vibrated on the bedside table, jarring Hugh Jack awake. His eyes blinked slowly trying to remain opened. With visions of Nickie still dancing in his head, he glanced over at number four. She barely moved despite the noise.

He stared at his wife and thought about Nickie. Hugh Jack ignored the normal things he sought in a wife when he met Sheila. She was not a beauty. Her religion didn't see the need for makeup. Her hair was kept at a certain length and wound in a tight bun on the back of her head. He struggled most with her weight and paid attention to the places they were seen together in public.

Those who knew Hugh Jack knew of his propensity for good looking young women, and had realized quickly that he married Sheila to maintain his connection to the practice of law.

He could accept her looks. He could even go to church with her on occasion. What he couldn't abide was her honesty and inability to look the other way or simply bend the rules a little. For her it was love; for him it was a marriage of convenience and necessity. A business transaction. It wasn't by chance that she just happened to be an attorney.

He sat up and swung his legs off the bed, resting his feet flat on the floor. His elbows propped on both knees as he planted his face in his hands; his palms rubbing his eyes. He sat staring into the darkness waiting for his eyelids to fully open. He reached his right hand over his left shoulder to scratch an itch and turned, looking out the window at the blackened sky.

Then, as if someone had flipped a switch, he remembered the bones. He jumped to his feet, but stood still for a moment to allow blood to flow south and slowly correct the inflammation. He walked gingerly until the pain subsided.

He quickly dressed in work clothes. He slipped on a pair of rubber boots that stopped just under his knee. He tightened the strap on top, anticipating the suction of mud, and headed toward the golf course.

Once in his truck, he realized the sun would not crest the pines for a while so he stopped at The Biscuit Palace for breakfast.

"Mr. Hugh, well look a there, I ain't seen you in a while, where you been?"

"Angie how you doin' Darlin'?" Hugh Jack asked, his deep, booming voice waking those who hadn't had their first sip of coffee yet.

He walked behind the counter and gave Angie a hug and grabbed a piece of bacon, biting into it.

"Extra crispy just like I like it, Darlin'."

Hugh Jack made his way toward the paper stand, picked up the weekly that had just been delivered only minutes earlier, and sat down in a cane bottom chair. The wood and cane moaned as they grappled under his large frame.

"Hugh you on the sports section yet?" Johnny Roy Woodson shouted across the room.

"Getting there now, Johnny Roy," Hugh Jack said as he turned the page. Hugh Jack was an anomaly in the State of Mississippi. He attended both rival colleges, but took no allegiance to one over the other. No fun could be had at his expense as the dog days of August bled into cooler September days and football season became the thrust of existence.

From now until January, men would talk of nothing else but football and hunting. Hugh Jack prepared himself to listen to Johnny Roy who knew every new player on both local high school teams. No report from Ole Miss ever escaped him.

"You see where Pop Jones boy's playin' quarterback over at the public school this year. Got everybody lookin' at 'em."

"Uh huh," Hugh Jack groaned, able to muster a quiet response between bites.

"They got a new boy over there this year, too, just moved down here from Tupelo, offensive linemen. That sumbitch weighs two eighty and stands six foot four, he's just a freshman, fifteen years old. That sumbitch's thighs are huge," Johnny Roy said, holding his hands in a circle showing the circumference of the boy's thighs.

Hugh Jack was reading the same article that Johnny Roy shouted across the room, spitting bits of egg and toast as he did.

"You see where Ole Miss has a kicker, they pulled out of a fraternity house, drunk off a keg? Coach heard he could kick, sobered his ass up, and gave him a football, kicking fifty yarders all day long. Sumbitch is fatter than I am,"

Johnny Roy said, laughing. "Goin' to school on scholarship now."

"Tell Hugh Jack about Jim Bell's boy," a faceless voice hollered.

"I watched the high school boys practice the other day. They got Jim Bell's boy playin' fullback. That boy is faster than greased owl shit. He hit the pock…"

Hugh Jack stood quickly after he took his last bite and downed one last drop of coffee. He walked over to Johnny Roy's table and grabbed his ticket.

"Got to get to work, Johnny Roy, I'll take care of this," Hugh Jack said, waving his ticket in the air.

"Now that's class right there," Johnny Roy said to only those that would listen.

"Angie, you outdo yourself every time, Darlin'," Hugh Jack said, as he laid a fifty dollar bill on the counter.

"He jus' never do shut up do he," Angie whispered in Hugh Jack's ear as he bent down to kiss her on the cheek.

"I've never known him to Darlin.'"

Hugh Jack placed his hat on his head as he left, Johnny Roy's voice fading behind the closing door, discussing Mississippi State and their new defense.

The rain had stopped sometime during the night. As he turned toward his barn, he switched to four-wheel drive again and slid as he turned onto the driveway. Mud kicked up in clumps onto the windows.

He exited the truck and quietly unlocked the door and made it to the back of his barn. Through those doors he walked along the edge of the fairway. He soon found himself standing in the dark at the bottom of the elevated number ten green, staring at the sky beginning to burn a hazy orange. The sun slowly pushed over the horizon. A light mist started falling. The clouds moved above as if they were angry and tired of being pushed around for three solid weeks by thunder, rain, and lighting.

He stood in the last place he remembered seeing the bones and stared into the dark woods. Its trees refusing the sunlight to pierce the thick canopy of leaves and limbs. He stared, wondering if whatever killed the person whose bones, he was now prepared to exhume was watching him.

Could it have been an animal? Could this be an old home-place; a family grave yard for the people that once inhabited these woods and cut a place to live out of the forest? Could they have died and been buried in the very place they made a life and a home?

As he stood leaning on his shovel, contemplating, the muddled sun gradually crested the tree line, introducing what looked to become a gray, hazy day. The sky blanketed with almost black clouds. He had no interest in giving himself away with a flashlight, and as the darkness began to dissipate, the ground before him began to show itself.

He moved into a better position. His feet were mired down into the mud and made a vicious sucking noise as he picked them up. Then came the familiar sound of gas escaping as he plunged them back down into his next step.

His eyes darted all over looking for anything that resembled bone. A good portion of the green grass now lay on top of the area where he first saw the remains the previous afternoon, and he slowly scraped away clumps of water-soaked grass.

The number ten flag lay buried with only the top portion protruding through the mud. He freed it, and as if he were throwing a javelin, hurled it back onto the remaining portion of the green. Four large scoops finally allowed his shovel to feel something with substance. He pulled at the mud, peeling back layer after layer until finally seeing the mud-filled eye socket of a skull.

He placed the shovel under it and gingerly raised it out of the mud. It was completely decapitated. He picked it up in the shovel, walked it back up to the top of the hill, and placed it on the portion of the green that was still intact.

Moving back to the same spot, he began removing mud above where the skull was found. Digging down close to a foot, he saw the top of the spinal cord. He frantically removed mud where he anticipated the rest of the skeleton to be and soon stared at the remains. It was positioned as it was buried as if dumped in the grave.

The corpse's mangled form sat slightly upward. Portions of a tattered shirt and pants were still visible and attached.

Hugh Jack placed the shovel under the remains as carefully as he could at different intervals, slowly heaving upward as he did, separating the bones from the thick mud. He finally had it free, and using the shovel, picked up the entire form and slowly pulled it out and across the ground so as not to disconnect the pieces. As he did, a rusted beer can fell back into the hole.

"That's an odd thing to bury with someone," he mumbled to himself.

As Hugh Jack looked at the skeleton, he realized it was not in a casket, nor was it dressed in a manner in which a loved one would be buried.

He loaded the remains onto a decoy sled attached to the rear of his four-wheeler and headed back to the barn.

Once inside, he hurriedly moved into the tack room and removed the tools and a chainsaw from a long wooden work table. He carefully placed the remains on top, grimacing as he touched them. He displayed them on the table replacing the head atop the spinal cord; then neatly arranged the arms by the side and the legs straight and together, just as one would see a cadaver in the morgue.

He filled a bucket with water, unwrapped a new three-inch paint brush and began removing mud. As he poured water on the remains and began brushing, the bones exposed a whiter color. Earth worms wiggled from hiding places. Spiders and ants made a mad escape as they felt their home intruded upon.

As more of the mud washed away and a full skeleton took a more discernable shape before him, Hugh Jack stopped what he was doing and walked about the barn and locked each door. He locked himself inside the tack room as well just in case Nickie made her way downstairs.

He again filled the bucket with water and poured it over the torso and lower arms. As mud flushed away, he noticed the left hand missing.

He grabbed the shovel and left the room, locking the door behind him. He reached the site and began digging in the location where the hand should have been based on how he found the body lying. He slowly scraped mud away and saw nothing.

"What the hell you doin', Hugh Jack?" a voice from the top of the green shouted. Ben Triplett, the greenkeeper, stood above him with a puzzled look on his face.

Hugh Jack panicked. *Think, Hugh Jack, think. This looks odd.*

"Oh, hey there Ben, I've been removing the trash from my drain pipe in the lake, just trying to see how stable this looks. Hope we don't lose any more of the green."

As Hugh Jack said this, he glanced down below where he stood and saw the other hand and a sparkle of gold. He moved in front of it to block Ben's sight.

"Looks like we'll have to get Russ back out here to repair this thing," Ben said as he made his way down toward Hugh Jack.

"I wouldn't if I were you, Ben, you'll get stuck and probably lose those shoes you have on, son."

"Yeah, you're probably right," Ben said, as he backed up.

"Who is Russ?" Hugh Jack asked.

"Russ Crawford. He owns Capstick Design Group. You remember. He and Bubba Stewart built this fairway extension and green back in the eighties, rededicated your marker," Ben said.

"Oh, of course, Russ, sure." Hugh Jack said still unsure of who he was.

"Well, I better be on my way. Just checking the course for damage. See ya' Hugh." Ben waved as he got back on his cart and headed down the fairway.

Hugh Jack turned around and gingerly, with his shovel, scooped up the hand and the gold lying near it. He trudged his way out of the mud-ravished grave and made his way back to the barn.

Careful to lock the door behind him, he let the hand slide into a bucket of water, slowly swirling it to remove as much mud as possible. As the mud cleared, he reached into the bucket and extracted a gold signet ring and rubbed the remaining mud from the initials. There was a large scripted *C* in the center, a scripted *R* on the left side, and another *C* on the right.

"RCC, C, Crawford, Russ Crawford." His face frowned with confusion and disbelief.

Hugh Jack checked the remaining pockets in the decayed pants searching for anything that might tell him whose remains lay before him. The two front pockets were rotted, unable to hold anything. He rolled the skeleton on its side and felt the back pockets, nothing on the left side, but he felt a lump on the right.

Carefully he pulled a wallet from the back pocket until he felt it begin to tear. The cotton fabric and leather from the wallet had grown into each other, becoming one over the years. He took his pocket knife and slowly cut around the rotted pocket. He placed it in the water bucket, separating the cotton from the leather. Pieces of paper disintegrated and flaked off. He picked up each one as they did and tried to read them, but they were clear as if they had never been written on. A folded piece of torn paper fell from a blob of mud, and using his knife, he easily worked the tip into one corner. After several painstaking minutes, the paper separated. He could only make out the handwritten letters "sto my mone," before carefully placing it to the side.

He kept probing the wallet until he felt what appeared to be a credit card. He dipped it back into the bucket and slowly brushed off the remaining mud and grime, extracting a card with a hard clear plastic protector. He dipped it into the bucket one last time, rubbing the mud from the plastic. As he did, he could make out the scripted word *Mississippi* on what appeared to be a driver's license. Rubbing the remaining mud, the laminated license was clear as day:

Randal Calhoun Crawford
Palm Breeze Apartments
1420 Ponce De Leon Road
Apt A-8
Biloxi, MS.39530

CHAPTER FIVE

Bubba Stewart walked down the long hallway that centered rows of offices and conference rooms at Capstick Design House. He walked past photos of Russ Crawford holding trophy after trophy, having won one golf tournament after another. The company employed twenty-five professionals in the golf course design field. Bubba oversaw the actual construction side of the business. Russ designed them, and Bubba built them.

Russ sat in the larger conference room with plans for a new golf course development spread out, completely covering the table. He studied the elevations for Indian Island Golf Course and Country Club, to be built on an island just south of Beaufort, South Carolina. The club house, tennis courts, two pools, and restaurant were being built atop the highest elevation on the main portion of the property. The complete development would be a master-planned community including a post office, grocery store, pharmacy, and clinic, just down the street from Indian Ridge School System.

The marina was to have one hundred and twenty boat

slips. One mile through the property they planned for a sporting clays course, complete with a world class quail hunting preserve.

Russ drew the plans and would construct the golf course as well as develop the sporting clays range and clubhouse.

Russ's business had done well since day one. And now with Bubba running the construction crews, something Russ had to oversee early on, the pace of the business picked up. After graduating from college in landscape architecture and golf course management, he played golf for a few years and then went to work for a major development company before starting his own firm. Since then, he has developed and built successful courses mainly in the southeastern United States.

Success found him early. After winning tournaments all over the South, his name was well known. Since then, his designs have been met with overwhelming excitement and approval.

After leaving the development company, he moved back to Lewiston, and hired Bubba to oversee his construction crews.

Tina Perry, Russ's secretary, buzzed the line in the conference room.

"Russ, you've got a call on line two."

"Can you take a message for me, Tina?" Russ asked, exasperated.

"It's Ben out at Beau Chene. He said it's urgent."

"Okay, I'll take it."

"Hello, this is Russ."

"Russ, Ben from Beau Chene. How you doin'?"

"Fine," Russ said curtly, trying to move the conversation along.

"Man, this rain we've been having has been something hasn't it?"

"Sure has. Tina said you have an emergency," Russ said, tapping his pen against the table.

"Oh yeah, we've had some erosion on one of the greens and have lost quite a bit of dirt work. The entire back half of the green is gone."

Tina walked into the room, and Russ motioned for her to give him a pen and a notepad.

"Russ, when do you think you could get somebody out here? You know we got that memorial tournament for Bud Triplett out here in three weeks."

"Ben, to tell you the truth, we are terribly backed up. We haven't been able to do much of anything with this rain. Hell, it's covered the entire Southeast. That tournament is in three weeks, you say?"

"Yes sir. I would normally let it slide and allow the players to just play a pin placement on the remaining portion of the green, but I'm afraid this is too unstable. Besides, we need your signature green to be ready for the tournament."

"My signature green?"

"Yes sir, number ten green. The one you and Mr. Bubba designed and built."

A silence fell over the phone. Russ, standing, fell back into his chair, his face white as if all blood had left his body.

"Are you okay, Russ?" Tina asked, noticing the loss of color in his face and the now blank stare.

"Hello, Russ," Ben said after a long silence.

"You said number ten?" Russ asked, swallowing hard.

"That's right, number ten, the dogleg left on the backside."

"Ben, be sure no one goes anywhere near there, could

still be very dangerous. There could possibly be a sinkhole. I'll be right out," Russ said, parsing his words, barely able to breathe.

"Will do. Thanks, Russ."

Russ dropped the receiver on the table, barely able to speak.

"Are you okay? What was that call about? Your face is white, and you're scaring me."

"Ah, ah, nothing, just some erosion from this rain out at Beau Chene. I'm heading out there now. Clear my calls and let anyone I have an appointment with today know I'll have to reschedule."

"Why don't you just let Bubba go?" Tina asked in a state of confusion.

Russ hurriedly left without saying another word. Once inside his truck, he realized sweat was pouring down his face ... a cold, nauseating sweat, the kind fear creates.

His foot laid flat on the accelerator. He bobbed and weaved through lunchtime traffic, driving out of frustration and fear. He stopped and started, cursing slow drivers who had nowhere to be at any certain time.

The first of the month brought folks to town from the county for shopping. *Of all days, why do all the country folks have to be here!*

Finally, breaking free from the town traffic and now on the highway, he floored the accelerator again. Driving thirty miles over the speed limit, he saw blue lights flash in his rearview.

Not considering that he was speeding, he imagined he must have already been caught.

"They've already found out," Russ said out loud.

In his mind, forensics labs had run tests, lab technicians had worked overtime. They knew who Randy was. They somehow traced it back to him while he was on his way to find the remains that no one should even be aware of yet. His ability to think clearly was affected by the sea of adrenaline that coursed through each cell in his body. He moved at warp speed toward the number ten green at Beau Chene. His brain spastic. His throat contracted as if a boa constrictor squeezed itself around him, forcing what air he had left to leave his lungs all at once. He felt as though he were hyperventilating, but having never done so, he was uncertain.

He pulled into the parking lot of a local restaurant, a converted gas station, and waited for the officer to make his way to the truck. It was taking too long. He could see him through the rearview mirror, no doubt calling in backup. With every second that ticked by, his heart beat faster. Thicker beads of sweat formed over his entire face. He could feel the hair over his ears dripping with perspiration. A bead of sweat slowly found its way down his back, now hot with fire.

The officer finally made it to the driver's side window.

"You got your license for me?" the young officer asked, nursing a mound of Skoal in his bottom lip, giving him a soft lisp.

Russ's hand shook as he extracted his license from his billfold.

"You alright? You don't look so good."

"Yes, officer, but I haven't been feeling well today," Russ said, as he reached in his console for a small hand towel and wiped his face.

"You aware you were going thirty miles over the limit back there?" the officer asked, as he slightly leaned to his right side and spit a long stream of brown juice through his lips.

"Sorry. Just trying to finish up on some work I'm backed up on."

The officer took a few steps toward his windshield to check his inspection sticker.

"I'll be right back," the officer said, staring at Russ again wiping his forehead.

The officer returned from his patrol car with Russ's license and a ticket.

"Slow it down, you hear?" Another stream of spit fell to the side where the officer stood and splattered on his boots.

Russ sat still for a second realizing he had to collect himself and calm down. He let out a hard pocket of air, finally put the truck in drive, and continued toward the golf course. He pulled up to the maintenance shed and began looking for a golf cart. Finding one, he threw a shovel, stakes, and caution tape in the back and headed for the number ten green. Halfway there, the cart started slowing, fading quickly, the batteries dying. He parked the cart in a row of trees, grabbed the shovel, stakes, and caution tape, and set off walking toward number ten.

Ben Triplett saw Russ walking across the fairway, arms full, and made his way to him. He pulled up behind him, calling his name at the same time.

Russ jumped, lost in his thoughts and focused on walking as quickly as he could. He never heard Ben approaching.

"We've got carts out here for you, man."

"I know. Just aren't fully charged," Russ said, pointing toward the dead cart.

"Hop in. I'll take you over there," Ben said, patting the seat beside him.

"Ben, I'd rather just go by myself. Since I'm here working now, it's a liability issue. I'm sure that ground is still unstable around the green." As soon as Russ said the words, he cringed to himself, realizing it was a poor excuse.

He was worried young Ben would see right through him, and he would be exposed. But to his surprise, Ben agreed, hopped out, and taking the shovel and stakes from him, put them in the back of his cart.

"I'll get that cart back to the maintenance shed and back on a charger. This one has a full charge on the batteries. You keep it as long as you need it."

"Thanks, Ben. I'm going to mark off the area. I'd appreciate it if you'd help me keep everyone away from there. It might not be a bad idea to place a sign at the number ten tee box that number ten is closed until further notice," Russ said, watching as Ben nodded his head, agreeing with every word.

Finally, Russ arrived at the number ten green. A flood of memories filling his mind. The last time he had seen the green torn up like that, he was digging the hole to bury his father in it. Memories of that night returned and filled his every emotion. The evolving years never eased the memories. Since that night, there was always that thing in his chest that never left, the repetitive tightening, the lump that wouldn't leave.

Russ timidly walked down the hill to the bottom of the green. He walked slowly, aware the speed that it took to get him here to the place he now stood wasn't important anymore. He struggled with having an almost reverent feeling now that he stood here. He needed to simply dig up the remains and hide them until he could come back for them in the dark of night.

Reality set back in as he started imagining where the body would lie. He looked above him and saw the now exposed white PVC water line he remembered installing just over a foot under the green's surface. He stood a little over six feet, and the water line was roughly four feet above where he stood.

As he continued to survey the area, he noticed the muddied footprints all around him. The prints of either dogs or coyotes covered the entire area. A small indention in the soil looked as though it could have at one time been a grave lay empty. What looked like shovel marks in the drying ground made his heart rate increase. A beer can sat rusted and dented. It was Randy's brand. Fear slowly replaced the reverence he first felt as he walked toward the grave, he had dug sixteen years earlier.

It was dark that night, but clear. He gaged the depth of the grave by how far the shovel of the backhoe reached into the earth. He remembered it was toward the back of the green where he now stood. Sure of himself, he frantically began to dig deeper and deeper down and then further toward the front. The sweat that had stopped and dried somewhat, now returning. The loose muddy soil fell away easily but ... nothing.

He stopped digging at the thought that dogs or coyotes may have dragged the remains away. He stared at the ground, hoping to see a direction to follow, but the tracks formed a circle at best. He began walking into the woods. They were thick with briars and deadfall. He searched until he found a game trail and followed it. He walked for what seemed like hours and found nothing. With each step his heart rate increased, and sweat flowed from his pores.

"If a dog or coyote dragged off a skeleton, surely parts would be found as they fell off. For that matter, surely a dog pulling at a skeleton out of thick mud would only be able to pull away a portion of it," Russ reasoned to himself out loud.

As he made his way back toward the green, his deep thought was interrupted.

"Man, who are you talking to?" Ben Triplett asked as he now stood in what was once a grave.

"Nobody. Just thinking out loud," Russ said, annoyed.

"Think we'll have to build some type of retaining wall on the back here to keep this from happening again?" Ben asked.

Russ's mind was not on work. He could think of nothing else but where the remains of his father might be.

"That's what I'm thinking, Ben," Russ said not sure what he was agreeing to.

"Y'all got any dogs out here, Ben?" Russ asked, pointing toward the ground.

"Yeah. Hugh Jack's bird dogs run up and down the fairway out here in the evenings. One of them must have got loose the other day. Hugh Jack was standing right in the middle of them tracks the other day, checking out the green. I think he thinks he owns this green since y'all gave him that marker with his picture on it, you know how he is," Ben said, as he watched the blood drain from Russ's face.

"You okay, Russ?" Ben asked as Russ turned, leaned on a tree, and vomited.

"Bad lunch," was all Russ got out. "I'll be okay," Russ said as he waved Ben off.

CHAPTER SIX

Hugh Jack sat in the small room that was now his office. It had been a hard fall from grace for him. At one time he had offices in four locations, all in Mississippi: Lewiston, Tupelo, Biloxi, and Greenwood. They were all opulent, large, well-appointed offices. Always sure to have a woman waiting for him as he traveled to each, making his rounds. Now he sat in what was once a small bedroom in an old house that served as the central office for Pest-B-Gone and his wife's law office. His wife's nephew owned and operated the pest management business, the shared office cut down on expenses for both.

His four-year-old female pointer, Trish, named after his last wife because she was also a bitch, sat tied to the desk leg, trying her best to stay away from Hugh Jack. Today she had an appointment with the veterinarian, but that wasn't why Trish avoided him.

Hugh Jack purchased Trish for one reason and one reason only ... to abuse.

Hugh Jack used Trish to obtain pain medication he was unable to get conventionally. His addictive personality landed him on every "drug seeker" list in every doctor's office in a one-hundred-mile radius of Lewiston. General practitioners, dentist, ear, nose and throat, anyone who could prescribe pain meds of any sort had turned Hugh Jack down time after time. He finally resorted to abusing Trish and hoping the pain meds worked on humans. His addiction to pain killers played a large role in losing his license to practice law.

Every month he took Trish to her veterinary appointment, kicking her in the left back leg on the way. She walked in limping. He needed her to whimper, to illicit a need for the drugs.

The plan worked as it had for the last several months, and as soon as he got in his truck, he popped in two of Trish's pills and started for his farm.

The earth was finally starting to dry. The rainwater that had filled ditches was receding, leaving water marks on the trees, dark from the soaking. The traffic was halted as a wrecker pulled a half-submerged Mini Cooper from a ditch. Water flowing from its interior as it was loaded onto the wrecker.

He finally broke free of the traffic and soon turned into the farm. He extracted a large leather suitcase from his back seat along with several towels from home. He walked Trish inside and into her pen.

Once inside the tack room, he locked the door behind him and made his way to the work table that held the remains. Reaching under the table, he opened a drawer and extracted the driver's license and other bits of papers. He placed them near the bottom at the end of the left hand, almost as if the skeleton were holding it. He took two photos with a Polaroid camera. He waved them in the air, waiting for the image to materialize from black. The license in the photo was clear. He opened the suitcase, lined the bottom with a towel, and placed skeleton parts inside as gingerly as possible. He laid a towel between the layers as he stacked the bones. He placed the license and wallet remnants in a small pocket in the suitcase lid, added the leftover towels on top to further pad it, closed it, secured the straps, and took it out to his truck.

Hugh Jack drove, contemplating a safe place to keep the suitcase. He drove to the office, quickly erasing that from consideration ... too many prying eyes. He drove to a storage business and thought about renting a unit, but didn't feel that was safe enough.

He drove out to his house and imagined number four finding the suitcase and he nixed that thought. Back in town he realized the safest place was at the barn. He was there every day and he had a good hiding place. The hidden room under the loft, near the guns, and what little cash is still there, would be the safest place.

He arrived back at the barn after driving by the office making sure that number four was there. He retrieved the suitcase from the back seat, made his way to the tack room, and walked to the false wall. He removed the three bales of hay that covered the secret door, lifted the floor plank, pulled the switch, then opened the door and placed the suitcase inside. It fit perfectly. He replaced the boards and added two more bales of hay to make himself feel better and was back at the office before lunch.

CHAPTER SEVEN

Russ stood in his mother's doorway, his body limp. Although William "Cappy" Capstick had been dead for several years, Russ still thought of him, especially in difficult times. He still needed his wisdom. Even now when he knew he couldn't talk to him, it would at least help if he could just talk about Cappy to someone who knew him well.

"Bud, you look rough. What's wrong?" his stepfather, Jim Spencer, asked. Russ's face was a pale white.

"Rough day," Russ said, as his chin quivered and tears worked themselves up from the depths of their ducts as a newly tapped oil well about to burst.

He held back the tears until his mother walked into the room. Then they began to flow. He fell to his knees, grasping his mother's waist, wailing. He was tired of the memory, the nightmares. He was tired of his father. Although he had been dead for sixteen years, he was still alive ... alive in Russ's memories ... the abuse, the hate-filled words, the drinking, the murder, the dreams, all of the dreams, and now his missing remains. He never stopped being. He continued to live even in his death.

"Have you ever told Jim?" Russ asked through broken sobbing.

"No, baby."

"Tell me what?" Jim asked, confused by Russ's sudden burst of emotion.

Jaimey looked as though she has been expecting such a day. Almost glad it had finally arrived.

"About the day my dad died. It's a story that I've held onto since that day. Moms held it in too. We were all a part of it. Me, mom, Bubba and Cappy. Bubba and Cappy took him off that night from the party. Before I tell you, I've got some questions about the night Cappy died. I'm afraid that his death was in part related to the night that dad died," Russ said.

"What do you need to know buddy?" Jim asked Russ, his eyes wide with worry.

"Tell me about when Cappy died," Russ said.

"You've never asked me that, why now?" Jim asked, confused.

"I just need to know."

Jim looked at Jaimey frowning, unsure of what this all meant.

"Okay … well, I was there as his doctor, making sure he was comfortable. Bubba showed up. You were on the way. It was the end, and he knew it. His breathing was labored. He had that faraway look in his eyes like he had had for months since the dementia set in. When Bubba got there, he halfway sat up in the bed and saluted him." Jim laughed a little remembering the salute.

"You know he always said Bubba looked like someone he

served with in Korea. But then, all of the sudden, he became very lucid. He started talking to Margaret, like he was actually having a conversation with her, and his eyes lit up. He almost had a sparkle in them. He reached out like he was touching something soft and sweet. He talked about you and Jaimey and asked me and Bubba to be sure we took care of you two. And then he asked Bubba to get some wine. We thought he just wanted one last drink, but then he couldn't tell us what to do with it. Bubba poured a small amount for him, then he pointed to us and pointed toward his mouth. Bubba and I looked at each other, confused, and he turned his head and stared for what felt like an eternity at his Bible and returned his gaze."

Jim's voice cracked, he had stop for a moment, but continued recounting the day.

"Bubba glanced at his Bible and then asked him if he wanted to take Communion and he nodded, relieved that he was finally understood. Bubba left to go get some crackers. Cappy wanted me to help him sit up. When Bubba returned, he began. First Bubba and I served each other, and then we broke off a small piece and placed it in Cappy's hand."

Jim stopped and let out a hard breath before he could continue. As if he were reliving the event in real time, he recounted almost word for word giving Cappy Communion.

"This is my body, broken for you," Bubba said. "Cappy's hands were shaking as he brought the cracker to his mouth. It took him a long time to swallow. His brain just wouldn't tell his body what to do."

Jim had to stop again. His face contorted in pain from the memory. He put a tight fist to his mouth and lightly bumped his lips trying to fight back the emotion.

"This is my blood spilled for you," Bubba said. And I

helped Cappy drink. He laid back down, roughly made the sign of the cross and let out a short burst of air. His mouth tried for a long time to form a word. He finally said "Margaret," and then he was gone. He had the most peaceful, serene look on his face. I knew he was seeing his wife again," Jim choked as he said the last sentence.

"Jim, I heard a news report last week that talked about people with dementia and how a particular event in their life could possibly trigger the disease, is that true?" Russ asked through a soft sob.

Jim looked at Jaimey, now covered in tears. She nodded as if to say *tell him.*

"Yes, that has been the result of some studies. Why?"

"Bubba told me recently that Cappy thought he killed Randy the night of the golf tournament, thought he beat him so bad that he went off somewhere and died because he was never found."

"He did wonder about that," Jim said to Russ unsure of where he was going with all of the questions. "What are you getting at Russ?"

Russ looked up at Jaimey and paced the floor back and forth. "Jim, I need you to leave the room."

"Russ what....," Jim was interrupted by Russ.

"You don't need to hear what I'm about to say to Mom. I don't want you involved," Russ said, wiping his face and dripping nose.

Jim left the room.

Russ turned to Jaimey, "The back part of the number ten green was washed away in the rain, I can't find the remains; they're gone," Russ said matter-of-factly, relieved to finally get it out.

Jamie fell onto the couch, her face expressionless and resolute. Silence filled the room for several seconds.

"Mom, I had no idea about Cappy until recently. I still couldn't have told him what I did. That would have killed him for sure."

"You had no way of knowing, Russ. You did what you had to do. Now we need to focus on getting them back," Jaimey said, trying her best to comfort Russ.

"You've looked? You're sure?"

"I'm positive, but I think I know who has them," Russ said, his voice stronger.

Jaimey's eyes widened.

"How do you know," Jaimey asked, surprised.

"Ben Triplett, the greenkeeper at the country club said Hugh Jack Rives was poking around the bottom of the number ten green. There were dog tracks as well as boot prints all over the area."

Jaimey rolled her eyes when she heard Hugh Jack's name.

"That means only one thing; he wants money. Everybody knows he needs it. But wait... how can he connect it to you?" Jaimey asked, hoping for no definitive answer.

"Mom, everyone connected to the country club knows Bubba and I built that green, and they can figure out when Randy went missing. It doesn't take a genius to figure out who killed him. It would either be me or Bubba, and I'm sure as hell not going to let Bubba's name get dragged through the mud on this," Russ said.

"Russ, we've got to tell Jim. You're going to need his help, and I can't continue to keep this from him any longer. It's eating at me too," Jaimey said.

"That son of a bitch just won't die. He just can't leave us alone," Russ said. "I've got to tell Bubba, too."

"Russ, I don't know. It's better not having too many people involved."

"I know, but he's my partner, and I'm going to need his help. You know he would never do anything to hurt either one of us."

"You're right. Call him over here. Let's get Jim back in here, too."

After a long pause, Russ agreed with Jaimey and nodded his approval.

In short order, Bubba arrived and walked through the back door to find all three of them sitting quietly at the kitchen table. Russ and Jaimey wore serious looks on their faces, and he could tell they had been crying.

"Russ, what's going on?" Bubba asked, eyes wide.

Russ stood and immediately rushed to the back door and vomited. He came back in, wiping his mouth, his face white from anticipation. He went to the kitchen sink and rinsed his mouth before wiping his face with a wet rag. Jaimey began to quietly weep.

"Oh God, is Will okay"" Bubba asked hoping nothing happened to Russ's son.

"He's fine, Bubba."

Russ walked over to the table, sat down, and immediately stood back up and began pacing again.

"What in the hell is going on? Would someone please tell me?"

"Yeah, I'd like to know myself," Jim said, staring at Jaimey.

Russ finally sat and stared at Bubba and Jim.

"It's about the night of the golf tournament after my father's blowup."

"Yeah, Cap and I took him to the barn and we beat his ass," Bubba said still looking confused.

"When I left you two and went for a ride," Russ said, "I went to the barn."

"Okay," Bubba said almost as a question.

"I had been through that very situation. Mom and I, I should say, we had been through that very situation a million times before. Embarrassed, hurt, mad, pissed off...."

Russ's voice trailed off as if he were lost in some deep memory.

"You name it, we've felt it all. Physically, emotionally, it hurts most deep down because that's where you keep it, buried ... in your gut."

Russ twisted his fist in front of his stomach to make a point, gritted his teeth when he did.

"When I got to the barn that night, he talked about how winning the golf tournament wasn't a big deal. I just wanted him to be proud of me. He told me again that night that he wished I had never been born. That was one of a million times he had said that to me. I flashed to his hitting mom, spitting on her, and turning his own wife out on the streets. The last thing he said to me was I wish you had never been born. Hate came out of him with everything he had. I had finally had enough. I picked up my driver, I straddled him and swung as hard as I could into the side of his head... and I killed him."

Bubba stood and slowly backed away from Russ, pacing the floor in the kitchen. The color had left his face as well. The four of them looked ghostly, shocked. Jim put his arm around Jaimey.

"That night," Russ said as he stood and looked directly into Bubba's eyes, "I killed my father and buried him under the number ten green at Beau Chene with your backhoe."

Russ and Bubba stood staring at each other. Two grown men wiping tears, hugging.

"Russ, if you have come to me for forgiveness or some sort of attestation, you already know you have it. I know what kind of man he was; neither of you deserved the way he treated you. I can't imagine carrying this with you all these years. Everything's going to be okay," Bubba said, as his face fought tears from returning.

"I feel the same way, bud," Jim said, hugging Russ.

"Thank you both for that, but there's more," Russ said as he looked at Jaimey. A long silence fell over the room.

"The back of number ten green has washed away from the rain; I can't find his remains."

"What do you mean you can't find them?" Bubba asked, a hint of nervous energy emanating from him.

"The remains are gone. I think I know who has them."

"Who?" Jim asked Russ.

"Hugh Jack Rives," Bubba interrupted with an air of certainty.

Everyone turned to Bubba.

"How the hell did you know that?" Russ asked, astonished.

"It's the only thing that fits. He's right there, he walks the fairway on number ten with his dogs almost every evening. It's been raining. No one else has been out there playing. He's the only person it could be," Bubba said, convinced he was right.

"Ben Triplett at the country club said he saw him at the bottom of the back of the green. He has them," Russ said sure of himself.

"And he'll be looking for a payday," Jim said throwing a napkin in the trash.

"Does he know that you know about the green being washed away yet," Jim asked.

"Not unless Ben mentioned to him that he was calling me out there. Why?"

"Well, we aren't one hundred percent sure that Hugh

Jack has the remains. I'm sure you're right, Russ, but what if you aren't? What if you confront him and he doesn't know? Now you've made him aware. I think it would be best if you just let him come to you. Hugh Jack will be looking for a payday. We all know he's flat broke. Let him send you the blackmail demands, and in the meantime, we can use that time to come up with a plan. Of all the people you want to have possession of something like this, it's Hugh Jack. He won't go to the police, and he needs the money."

Jim's reasoning made sense.

"So now that all this is out, I need to know truthfully how this changes your feelings about me. Bubba are we good, are we going to be able to continue to work together?"

"Russ, as far as I'm concerned you survived that night and protected your mother. You probably should have done it sooner. Hell, I wanted to kill him that night myself. Cappy did, too. I love you, buddy; this doesn't change a thing."

"I'm only sorry you had to carry this all these years, Russ. I know this was hard telling us, I wish you could have told us sooner," Jim said, still in shock.

"He was irredeemable," Jaimey said. Looking at Jim, her eyes filled with tears.

CHAPTER EIGHT

Nickie walked out of the apartment and stood at the top of the stairs in a pair of panties and a New Orleans Saints jersey with no bra on. Hugh Jack was in the tack room counting money and placing it in a small duffle bag.

"What the hell are you doing down there?" Nickie asked, as she lit a cigarette and blew out the smoke.

Hugh Jack walked out of the tack room, "Darlin' you can't smoke in here. With all this hay, this place will be consumed by fire in no time."

Nickie rolled her eyes and dropped the butt in her coffee cup.

"You're too young to be smokin' anyway," Hugh Jack said, surprising himself at the fatherly advice.

He had always known he was too selfish to have any children of his own. The vasectomy he had between his graduation from Mississippi State and the year he entered Ole Miss had a lot to do with his first two divorces. They both wanted babies, neither were fit to be parents.

For some reason Hugh Jack was always attracted to

trashy women, never women who would make good mothers. The trashier, the better for him. He loved the way trashy women dressed, how they applied their makeup, and the cheap perfume they sprayed all over their bodies ... the gaudier the better.

All that added up to sex. Trashy women just meant sex, and besides personal injury law, sex is what he thought about the most part of every day.

He had noticed Nickie and the way she was dressed, and he did something he couldn't believe when he did it. He told her to go put some clothes on. He couldn't understand what this girl held over him. Normally he would have already been upstairs and out of his clothes. She almost had some strange power over him.

Considering her age, had he not known the vasectomy had worked all those years ago, he would have almost wondered if she could be his daughter from some trashy, horrid affair.

He needed her to leave so he could hide the duffle bag back in his secret room. She turned to go back into the apartment, and he watched her ass when she did. He shook his head.

"Damn son," he said with a crooked smile, out loud to no one.

Before Nickie was out of full view, she noticed Hugh Jack hurriedly move back into the tack room. She heard him shut the door and lock it. Then almost just below her feet, she heard a door squeak, some shuffling, and a door quietly close. She then heard him coming back through the tack room door, and she quietly closed her door.

"I'll see you later Darlin'!" he said as she heard one of the large front doors screech open.

"Bye," she hollered.

She quickly got dressed, put on some tennis shoes, and made her way downstairs. She walked over to the large double doors and slightly opened them and peered out. He was gone.

She walked to the tack room and tried the door, it was locked. She walked back up to her room, got a bobby pin from her small makeup bag, and returned to the tack room.

She inserted the pin into the lock and worked the tumblers, she felt them move and before long, the door was unlocked and she was walking through it.

She turned on the light. The room was full of dog leashes and leads. Reins for horses hung from the wall. Two saddles sat on saw horses at the end of the room. There was something covering all of the walls in the room except one —the wall to the left as you walk in. The same area where Hugh Jack opened and closed a door, but it was just a solid wall. Nothing hung on it, nothing stood along the wall except hay bales; and nothing was propped on it. It was just a plain wall. There was no door, no shelf, no nothing.

She walked to the door she had just come through, and opened it and closed it. No squeak. She worked it back and forth. Nothing. She walked along the walls on the other side of the room, inspecting them closely. Nothing. She walked around the small room twice and stopped, thinking she heard something. She ran out of the room and toward the large entrance doors, peaking out of the crack, but it was just the garbage men.

She made her way back to the tack room and sat down on a bale of hay looking around, thinking of where the noise came from and stood. As she did, she heard a click that sounded as if it came from under the hay bale. She moved the hay and stepped on a floor plank watching one end pop up. She bent down and brushed away the loose hay and pulled the plank up completely. Looking under it, she saw a metal ring attached to a wire. It looked as if it was floating in mid-air. She slid her finger through the ring and pulled. When she did, the wall in front of her almost hit her in the head. She heard the familiar squeak, she was in.

She opened the "wall" completely and looked in. There were guns lined up along the back of the cubby hole. On the floor in front of those were duffle bags stacked on top of a large leather suitcase. She opened one of the duffle bags and her eyes widened.

"Holy shit," she sang as she grabbed a bundle of cash and held it.

She zipped that bag and unzipped another. She heard Hugh Jack outside calling one of his dogs as they all started barking. She closed the bag, stuffed the cash down her pants, closed the door, hearing it click, and replaced the flooring plank and the hay bale. She crept out of the door, making sure it was locked and started up the stairs toward the apartment. She hid the money in her things and met Hugh Jack coming through the door as she descended the stairs.

CHAPTER NINE

Hugh Jack sat at his desk in his claustrophobic office. He felt certain his current desk must have come from Wal-Mart. His previous desks from each of his offices were sold at auction for a fraction of what he paid to have them built.

A startup law firm out of Montgomery, Alabama, bought the desks for five thousand apiece. He remembered paying twelve thousand each. When he commissioned them to be built, his only request was that the desk be high enough and long enough to comfortably fit a woman under it while he sat conducting business.

Meeting after meeting he sat with a one-hundred dollar per hour "secretary" under the desk earning her money while clients sat across from him. The secretaries were good at their job, finishing and zipping him up, just in time, so he could stand and walk his clients out of the office. His clients never suspected a thing. If the new owners knew what secrets those desks held, they wouldn't believe them.

Today however, he sat at a cheap desk that probably

cost as much as the secretaries made every two hours. The pressboard edges were chipping. His knees hit the bottom of the center drawer, and every time he opened the file drawer on the right side, it fell apart. He always forgot and had to spend fifteen frustrated minutes rebuilding it before it would shut.

As he sat there reminded of how far he had fallen, the amount kept rising.

"How much do you charge to return the bones of a murder victim to the murderer? The real question is, how much is the murderer's life worth to him out of prison?" He mumbled to himself.

There wasn't a secretary available to write the message. Even if there were, he couldn't trust anyone with that information.

He placed the first, second, and third trial runs of the letter in the heavy metal waste basket. A left-over remnant from the second world war. He struck a match and threw it in and watched the edges start to turn black. He opened the only window in his office and set the trash just under it and watched the smoke rise and filter to the outside.

"Hugh Jack, you burning something?" Sheila asked through the door. She tried opening the door but was unable to.

"Everything's okay! Just lit a cigar and forgot I wasn't supposed to smoke inside the office. Just put it out. I've got the window open, sorry," Hugh Jack shouted through the door.

His brain filtered through one idea after another as to how to make the exchange. The wording of the letter still uncertain in his mind. He was reminded of a movie he saw once. A bag of money was being paid for ransom. The instructions were that the money had to be placed in a garbage can. The can had been placed over a manhole cover on a sidewalk and had a false bottom in it. The bag was dropped into the can, it fell right through to the waiting blackmailer below the street, and off he went. No one was the wiser as he ran right under them making his escape and popping back up just outside an abandoned building.

The problem with that was there were no manholes on the sidewalks in Lewiston, Mississippi.

"I couldn't fit my fat ass through a manhole to begin with," Hugh Jack said out loud.

"Who are you talking too in there?" Sheila asked.

"Are you just standing outside my door, do you need something?"

"No," Sheila said with a saddened tone in her voice. He heard her as she walked away and shut the door to her office.

Hugh Jack jotted notes on a yellow legal pad. He wrote the word "RANSOM" in capital letters and the number fifty thousand and circled it several times.

"Hell, I'd pay a hundred grand to keep my ass out of prison."

He flipped to the page where he started the next letter and marked through the fifty and wrote *one hundred thousand dollars*. His chair squeaked as he leaned back and propped his feet on the desk. He stared at his boots and realized they cost more than the furnishings in his piece-of-shit office. He was tired of this place—the smell of pesticides, other chemicals, the rap music blaring every time a truck returned from spraying for the day. His stepdaughter always wanting money, threatening to tell her mother about *that* time.

He tapped the pen on his lips, thinking ... thinking of a drop-off point, thinking how he could communicate to Russ where the remains were, thinking every point, thinking how the exchange would take place.

As he rested his head on the back of his chair and stared at the ceiling for inspiration, vibrations followed by the loud thump and beat of distorted speakers returned his psyche to the reality of the current hell he lived in. The music that thumped in his head reminded him of The Purple Palace.

The Purple Palace was a juke joint housed in an old warehouse that Hugh Jack owned in the seventies through the mid-eighties. He leased the building to Tyrone Suggs, a local entrepreneur and bookie. Hugh Jack gave him a heavily reduced rate on rent if he would cut him in on the numbers action. Since Lewiston was dry, Hugh Jack supplied him with booze, store bought, as well as shine. Also, with his connections, Hugh Jack kept the cops away from the door. It was a win/win for both, and they both made plenty of money. The Purple Palace eventually closed years later when the booze was replaced with cocaine, and the ATF showed up unannounced and shut the place down.

When it was at its prime however, the music, light show, and entertainment were all top notch.

The warehouse originally served as a storage building for a wholesale grocery company. The ceiling held two large platforms that were raised and lowered by a pulley system, used for loading pallets of dry goods and storing them on the second floor. It also served as a cool way for band members at The Purple Palace to descend from the ceiling amid smoke and a laser light show that rivaled *Soul Train* any day of the week.

As Hugh Jack remembered the band members descending onto the stage, he knew how they would make the switch. Two platforms, one for the money, the other for the bones. He would never be seen.

"That is how we'll do it," he excitedly muttered under his breath.

Hugh Jack walked out of his office placing his cowboy hat on his head and fell into his Mercedes. The warehouse was only a mile away. He pulled into the parking lot and made his way around back to the still vacant building. An addition had been added since he owned it.

Since the bypass was built on the outskirts of town, old buildings sat vacant and unused all over town. He tried the doors in the back, sure to stay away from prying eyes near the front. He broke a single pane on the side door, reached his hand inside, and unlocked it. Once inside, he noticed the addition had two large double doors that would allow him to pull his truck inside.

He walked the stairs that led to the second floor and to a balcony. He made his way up and walked through a door that led into the room with the two platforms.

He physically moved the platforms to be sure they still worked. He walked through the exchange, moving as he would that day, making sure he would never be seen.

With the logistics planned for the exchange, he sped back to the office, sat down, and finished writing the letter. The paper crinkled as he fished the end through the roller on the typewriter crooked. He backed the paper out and fished it back through again straightening it. He glanced at his yellow legal pad and pecked with one finger each word he had written. The slow rhythm of the typewriter echoing throughout the office.

"Are you typing in there?" Sheila asked.

"Dammit will you leave me alone, I'm trying to get some work done."

A very quiet "sorry" answered him.

The letter zipped through the roller as Hugh Jack finished. He read over it one last time before placing it in a manila envelope.

```
I believe I have something you want.
Follow these instructions:
Bring one hundred thousand in cash to the
warehouse located at 1233 West Main Street.
The front door will be unlocked. Enter
there. Once inside, you will see a platform
on the ground. Another will be suspended
just above your head with your package on
it. Place your bag on the empty platform.
As I raise that platform, the other will
lower. It will be an even trade. The
exchange will take place two weeks from
this date at 6:00 P.M. No cops, no one
with you.
```

Hugh Jack added the photos of the license and the bones and took out the photo of the signet ring, since he decided to melt that down for the gold. He shoved them in the envelope, closed it with the metal clips, and taped it for good measure. He tore the handwritten letter along with three sheets behind it just in case he bore down too hard with his pen and threw them in the trash can again. He placed the garbage can just outside his office window and threw a match inside. He watched as the paper turned from yellow to black.

Lewiston was dead and dark. Main Street always was shortly after five. Hugh Jack pulled up on the corner beside the Capstick Design House, walked quickly to the front door, slid the package through the mail slot, and more quickly returned to his car and sped away.

CHAPTER TEN

Nickie walked along South Columbus Avenue toward town on her way to get a small bag of groceries and hopefully find someone who would sell her some marijuana. The closest country store was almost a half mile away. As she arrived, only one car sat in the parking lot. The possibility of buying something to smoke didn't look too promising.

As she walked in, the young boy behind the counter interrupted his conversation and spoke to her. He was talking to an old man in overalls, who sat reclined next to an old pot belly stove with his fingers laced across his small belly. He coughed hard and long, spitting into a rusted Folgers coffee can beside his right foot.

Nickie was immediately disgusted by the old man, as she walked close to him to get a coke from the cooler. An older woman appeared out of the lady's room and took her place by the old man.

Nickie felt them both staring at her like they wanted to ask her something, whispering between themselves.

She had been the stranger many times in her young life.

Regardless, it made her uncomfortable, and as she paid for her groceries and walked out of the door, she heard them move their chairs, stand, and start following her.

She quickened her pace as she glanced over her shoulder and saw them follow her outside.

"Hey young un," the man said as he hurried toward her with his hand up in the air as if hailing a cab.

"What the hell do you want?" Nickie asked, as she turned and stood with her pocket knife held out in front of her.

The old man stopped in his tracks and reached in his shirt pocket and withdrew a joint.

"I've got pot," he said, twisting the joint between his fingers.

"What makes you think I want that?" Nickie asked.

"You smell like weed," the old man said.

The woman stood behind the man, holding the wrist that was propped on her hip, staring at Nickie, hoping she would buy a joint from them.

"Who are you?" Nickie asked, shocked. They didn't look like your normal dope peddlers.

"He's Bandit and my name's Honey, spelled H u n y not H o n e y,", the woman said spelling her name slowly for Nickie.

Huny was shorter than Bandit. Her hair was greasy, had not been washed or combed for what appeared to be days. Her jaw jutted out beyond her top lip, and she had no teeth. Her eyes were deep set and framed underneath by dark circles, wearing a look of defeat. When she spoke, she whistled.

"Where's that from?" Nickie asked.

"Growed right here out in the country, original seeds brought to Mississippi all the way from Brazil on a plane back in the seventies, how many you want, hun?" Bandit asked.

"How many you got?"

"Ten rolled and a bag of loose. Four of the rolled are spoken for though, so six joints."

"I'll take it," Nickie said, as she reached into her pants pocket and extracted the roll of cash.

"Which one?" Huny asked.

"All you got."

Nickie handed the man a one-hundred-dollar bill.

"This shit is from Brazil, it'll be two hundred," Bandit said eyeing the cash in Nickie's hand.

Normally Nickie would have argued, but the cash came easy, and she knew where there was more of it.

"You need help burnin' 'em down?" Huny asked.

"We coasted into the parkin' lot on fumes, but now that we got some cash to fill up, we can give you a ride. Where you live, hun?" Bandit asked.

"Just up the road about a half mile, but I can walk," Nickie said sheepishly, thinking of carrying all the pot she just purchased and the highway patrolman that passed her on her way to the store.

"Hell, we can give you a ride. Ain't that right, Bandit?"

"We can now that we got some gas money. Come on. Hop in."

Nickie slid in the back seat. After several attempts to crank his van, it finally fired up and Bandit pulled up to the gas pump and pumped five dollars' worth. Back in the car, he turned left out of the parking lot.

"Where we goin'?" Nickie asked, as she fumbled in her purse past all of the pot, feeling around for her knife again.

"There's a lake resort just down the way, I need to go deliver some weed to some kids. It's just about a mile.

Won't take but a minute," Bandit said, as he continued toward the lake.

"Well, okay, but I need to be gettin' on back."

As soon as she said that, the lake came into full view. Two Antebellum houses stood on opposite hills overlooking the lake.

Bandit eventually turned right into a parking lot. In front of them was a two story sixty-four-unit motel. He drove around the back of the motel eventually hitting a gravel road.

"Where we heading?" Nickie asked, as she placed one hand on the door handle and tightened the one around the pocket knife in her purse.

"They's some RVs right through here, these kids stay in," Huny said as she pointed in front of them.

Something about Huny's face looked honest to Nickie. Bandit parked his car in front of the small RV. The RV was pulled by a rusted van with stickers, covering their entire back glass, revealing every concert the owners had attended for the last three years.

Bandit blew the horn, and a young man and woman walked out of the door rubbing their eyes as if they had just awakened from a nap. They both wore dreadlocks, and their bodies were covered in tattoos. Neither of them wore a shirt. The girl sat on the steps and lit a cigarette, continuing to rub her eyes. She scratched her arm pit that had not been shaved moving to her ankles that were red from bug bites.

Bandit and the man made the exchange, and Nickie watched as the man hit the woman on the rear as they giddily made their way back into the travel trailer.

Bandit circled around the travel trailer and made his way back to the gravel drive, and back onto the main road that led them away from the resort.

A black Corvette turned onto the road behind them. As they neared the convenience store, Nickie finally felt relieved and no longer worried that she was being kidnapped.

Bandit slowed at the stop sign and turned right. The Corvette held back but turned in behind them.

"It's right up here on the left, right there," Nickie said pointing toward Hugh Jack's barn. "Keep going! Keep going!" Nickie shouted, seeing Hugh Jack's Mercedes parked at the barn. She slid down into the seat further.

Bandit weaved back onto the road, kicking up red dust. He came to a stop sign intersecting the bypass and turned right.

"What the hell was all that?"

"I ain't supposed to be bringing nobody to the barn. Take me back to the store and drop me off," Nickie said, her voice trembling.

Bandit made the big circle and arrived at the store.

"If you need any more weed you know where to find us," Huny said, pointing toward the store.

"All right. Thanks, y'all."

Nickie started walking back to the barn. Hugh Jack passed her and turned around and pulled into a driveway nearest her. He leaned over and opened the passenger door. As he did, the black Corvette passed by them slowly.

CHAPTER ELEVEN

Russ and Bubba arrived at the office at the same time and heard a package rustle behind the door as it opened. It wasn't unusual for packages to be delivered at odd times by couriers. Customers were constantly sending modifications to their plans and returning them to Capstick Design. Russ and Bubba usually had several projects in the works at one time.

"Hopefully that's the modification on the Quail Run Course," Russ said, as he bent down to retrieve whatever had been dropped.

The outside of the envelope was labeled;

For Russ Crawford Only.

Russ and Bubba stared at each other.

"The remains?" Russ questioned.

He hurriedly removed the tape across the flap and opened the metal clips on the package.

Russ pulled out one sheet of paper and two photographs paper-clipped to each corner. Bubba stood and walked to the door, closing it, although he knew they were alone in the office.

Russ disconnected the Polaroids from the paper, his hand shaking as he saw the photo of his father on his driver's license and then the photo of his skeleton. The juxtaposition of the two photos, flesh versus bone, was sobering.

"I still hate this son of a bitch."

"He wants to do the exchange at the old grocery warehouse," Bubba said, as he read the short instructions.

"When?"

"Two weeks from today."

"Why in the hell is he dragging this out two weeks, what's the purpose in that?" Russ questioned Bubba.

"He may have thought you would need that much time to raise a hundred grand."

"What, let me see that!"

Russ stared at the instructions.

"Where the hell am I going to get that much money?"

"We've got that in the construction account, don't we?" Bubba asked, almost scared of the answer.

"We have much more than that, but that's not my money, it's the company's. It's yours. We need that money to function." Russ said, almost dumbfounded at the amount.

"Let's stop and take a deep breath. Who are we dealing with here ... Hugh Jack Rives, who is really nothing more than a low-level, womanizing thug who happened to at one time be a practicing attorney. We both know this is knee jerk for him. He hasn't thought this through. Let's just come up with a plan. We'll work the problem through. We'll use the two weeks to our advantage," Bubba said, reassuring Russ.

Russ stared at the photo of Randy's driver's license.

"I was so angry that night, I couldn't think straight. It never occurred to me to check his pockets for I.D.," Russ said.

"Well, that just proves yours was a crime of passion. No premeditation," Bubba assured him.

"I can't tell you I never wished he weren't dead."

"Yeah, but that's a far cry from planning and executing a murder."

"Bubba, I'm so sorry for dragging you into this, but I'm glad you're here."

"Russ, I don't blame you for what you did. I can't imagine how you put up with the abuse all of those years, plus watching what your mother went through."

"Bubba, Jim told me Cappy thought he may have killed Randy and that may have led to his dementia." Russ said. "Did Cappy think he killed him?"

"Russ, Cappy beat the shit out of Randy. We both went back to the barn later that night, and he was gone. He knew y'all lived close to the golf course and thought he simply walked home. When he didn't surface in a few days, he thought he must have killed him. The only thing he couldn't figure out is where he wound up, so we thought he went off somewhere and died from his wounds," Bubba said, as he watched Russ wipe tears from his face.

"I kept reminding Cappy that I got in some pretty good licks that night, too. That seemed to make him feel better. You know, Russ, Cappy had a hard life. He fought in two wars and experienced more loss than most people do. That could have just as easily contributed to his dementia."

"I wish I had known. I would have told him. I would have told him what I did. As hard as that would have been, I would have told him," Russ said, as he took a deep breath.

They sat in silence unsure of what to say next. Russ sat back in his chair and stared at the ceiling.

"We have to get his remains back. If not, Cappy may have died in vain," Russ said.

Russ and Bubba immediately went to work. Bubba's fifteen years as a Marine in force reconnaissance replaced the golf course construction developer side of him, and he went about establishing a plan.

Bubba walked over to the courthouse and pulled up the last permit and blueprints for the warehouse. He also pulled court records which showed Hugh Jack's criminal charges and disbarment from the State of Mississippi.

Bubba sat back at the conference table with all of the papers spread out before them.

"Look at this. This building was at one time a used car dealership. They added this garage on the back. I'll bet you anything he has chosen this location so he can back his truck in there, unseen, and leave quickly after the exchange is made. We need to get over there tonight and take a look inside that building," Bubba said, as the plan began to develop.

CHAPTER TWELVE

The Corvette pulled in across the street from the barn and into a clump of trees. The occupants watching and waiting for Hugh Jack's Mercedes to pull into the driveway. The two brothers who sat inside were not only two low level dope pushers that Hugh Jack purchased Xanax and Mollys from, but two of his former clients as well. The Xanax was for him; the Mollys were for his unsuspecting dates.

Turtle McCowan and his brother, Peat, sat in the vibrating car as Marilyn Manson screamed hate-filled lyrics. The entire back end of the Corvette pulsed with speaker equipment. They sat in the car playing air drums, thrusting their heads backwards and forwards to the satanic beat while finishing a joint between them and believing every word from Manson's mouth.

Turtle's name came from his vocation. Along with being in the drug trade, he hunted turtles. He made soup with their meat, sold some to fishermen, and made jewelry from their shells. He mainly enjoyed torturing and mutilating them, boiling them and cutting them up before they were dead.

His brother Peat was a pyromaniac. He enjoyed burning anything he could get his hands on. Peat stuttering resulted in his nickname, Repeat. Over the years, the name had been shortened simply to Peat, mostly out of laziness.

Peat wore a scar from a bad burn on the right side of his face after he poured diesel fuel on a squirrel and lit it on fire just to watch it burn. Instead of running away, the squirrel jumped on Peat, scampering up the right side of his face and down his torso.

The brothers each served time in Parchman Prison and had been in and out of the county jail so many times they had lost count. The thought of murder didn't interest Turtle and Peat. Torture was their thing. If the truth were known, they were just too scared to kill anyone. The only thing they learned while spending time at Parchman farm is that they didn't want to go back.

In his spare time, Peat liked to sit in the middle of a lake, smoke a joint and dream up ways to torture people. Usually, he sat waiting in his Jon boat for Turtle to rise from the depths of the murky stagnant water with a fresh catch.

Turtle straightened in his seat as the Mercedes turned into the entrance to the barn. They watched Hugh Jack help Nickie with grocery bags and walk into the barn. Turtle reached into the back seat, retrieved his nine-millimeter, and handed the sawed-off shotgun to Peat. Neither was loaded.

As soon as the door closed, Turtle yelled above Manson singing a song of death and lost hope.

"Let's go."

He turned the car off. They looked around them before making their way out of their cover and sprinted across the road toward the barn. Once they reached the barn, they burst through the door and were on top of Nickie and Hugh Jack, pushing Nickie to the ground and thrusting the butt of the shotgun into the side of Hugh Jack's head.

The dogs barked, dancing from foot to foot, sneering at the two intruders.

Turtle pointed the nine-millimeter toward the line of dogs. "Shut your dogs up or I'm going to start shooting them one by one," Turtle said, as he kept the gun pointed toward the kennels.

Hugh Jack spoke a command to the dogs, and they went silent.

Turtle threw Peat his gun and wailed away on Hugh Jack's head. Kicking him in his gut, he placed his black combat boots squarely against his stomach. He rolled Hugh Jack over onto his back, punching him in his kidneys. Manson's words reverberating through his brain, calling for pain, torture, and revenge.

With every kick to the gut, turtle thought of the money that Hugh Jack stole from his father. Memories of the pain his father endured trying to hold on to life, until he knew his boys were going to be taken care of, fueled his rage even more. Turtle knew the pain and worry was the fault of one man, and he now had his boot sunk deep into his fat gut.

"I know the deal you made. I know you got a bigger settlement than you told us about. The lawyer explained to me what a class action lawsuit was. We ain't no class action, it was just Daddy. We want Daddy's money. He died all by hisself; didn't nobody else die!" Turtle screamed at Hugh Jack.

"Wwhere's our Dddaddy's money?" Peat stuttered holding Nickie by her ponytail as she knelt beside him.

"What money? I paid you fifty thousand apiece. Besides

my attorney fees that's all there was," Hugh Jack said, his words broken, almost unclear from the pain.

Nickie looked at him, knowing there was enough money in the secret room to take care of whatever debt he owed these two.

"Word I've been told is you made almost two million off my Daddy's case," Turtle said. "This looks like a good place to hide money to me."

"If I had it, you think I'm going to hide that much money in a barn?" Hugh Jack asked, shocked at how he knew about the money and the amount. *Who the hell told them?*

Hugh Jack had been double crossed. The frat boy attorneys didn't like him. He had humiliated and outsmarted them. In his mind, he had them all lined up in front of him remembering their faces, already working out revenge.

"Assholes," Hugh Jack thought to himself.

"The man told me you'd have to hide it cause most of it was paid under the table and got illegal, so yeah, I do. Where is it?"

"Our dddaddy tttrusted you," Peat said slowly.

Turtle sent Peat to search the barn for a hiding place. Peat handed Turtle his shotgun and he quickly began the search.

Hugh Jack listened as Peat turned over tables. He saw his favorite saddle fly through the tack room door. Tools were taken off the wall and thrown.

After almost thirty minutes, Peat returned, unable to find anything.

"I don't have a secret hiding place," Hugh Jack said.

"Maybe you know," Turtle turned to Nickie and placed the shotgun under her quivering chin. She almost blurted it out, but Hugh Jack spoke up.

"Look, Turtle, how do you know the person who told you this told you the truth," Hugh Jack asked, attempting to plant seeds of doubt in Turtle's mind. "You know, of all people, I have a lot of enemies out there. Don't you think someone could easily create a story like that and …"

"Shut up," Turtle screamed, as he pulled a newspaper clipping out of his shirt pocket, popped it open, and held it in front of Hugh Jack's face.

Hugh Jack read the headline: Lewiston attorney under investigation. He read enough of the lead sentence to know they had correct information. Bud McCowan's name was listed as Plaintiff. The accident, the money under the table, it was all there.

How the hell did they find out?

"Look boys, that article just isn't true. I'll give you back my attorney fees, ten thousand dollars. You boys can split it, five grand apiece."

"Now Hugh Jack, why would we want ten thousand dollars when we are owed so much more?" Turtle asked.

"Let's go," Turtle said, pointing the nine-millimeter at the two of them and walking them toward the front door. "This is your last chance, tell us where the money is."

"You gon' shoot me over ten thousand dollars, Turtle?"

"Oh, we ain't gon' ssshoot you, we just gon' mmmake you wish you was dead," Peat said.

Turtle threw the keys to the Corvette at Peat and told him to meet them at the compound. He forced Hugh Jack into the front driver's side seat of his Mercedes. He and Nickie sat in the backseat with a gun trained on Hugh Jack's head.

They turned off the main road behind the Corvette and followed Peat to the McCowan compound. Finally arriving, they drove into the center of three small buildings and parked beside a flag pole. A large Confederate flag waved in the light warm breeze. On the right side were three skinning poles where two large snapping turtles hung, waiting for the meat to be separated from the shell. Crushed beer cans overflowed from a rusted fifty-five-gallon drum, littering the ground around the skinning poles. Flies filled the air, while maggots feasted on the remains of a discarded turtle. The smell of rotting flesh hung in the air like thick molasses.

Turtle quickly had Hugh Jack and Nickie out of the car and standing in front of the Mercedes.

"Undress," Peat said to them, smiling at Nickie.

"Do what?" Hugh Jack asked, looking toward Turtle for answers. "What the hell is this really all about Paul?" Hugh Jack asked, calling Turtle by his given name.

"You can tell us where your money is or you need to get undressed. Get your clothes off!" Turtle yelled cocking the hammer and raising the pistol inches from Hugh Jack's face.

"Why me, dammit?" Nickie asked growing increasingly nervous.

"We're gonna torture Hugh. We just want to see you without no clothes on."

"Now," Peat said as he and Turtle both stood pointing their respective guns at the two of them.

Hugh Jack slowly started unbuttoning his shirt. He removed his cufflinks at the same time he squeezed out of his boots. He dropped his cufflinks into his boots. He took out his wallet and started to drop it in his boot as well but was stopped by Turtle who motioned for him to hand it over.

"There's six hundred dollars in there. That's it."

"I'll take it," Turtle said.

Hugh Jack removed his pants and stood in front of Nickie only in his boxer shorts.

"Everything. Get those boxers off and the socks."

Hugh Jack finished undressing and stood directly in front of Nickie, completely nude with the exception of his cowboy hat. They stared into each other's eyes.

"I'm sorry, Nickie," Hugh Jack said. "Darlin', I'm sorry I pulled you into this."

"Nnnow it's your turn," Peat said as he looked at Nickie and smiled, showing sparse yellowed teeth that had rarely been brushed.

"Please just leave her out of it. You've got me."

"Like I sssaid, we just want to see her without nnno clothes on."

Nickie slowly undressed, wondering to herself why she just didn't blurt out that she knew where the money was. But she wasn't sure that was all they were after.

Turtle and Peat both stared at Nickie until Turtle poked Hugh Jack in the back to move him down a path beside one of the trailers. They made Nickie walk behind Hugh Jack so they could watch her. They came to a small clearing in the woods. Nailed between two pine trees eight feet from the ground was a two by eight board.

Peat threw a rope over the top while Turtle placed zip ties on Hugh Jack's wrists. While Turtle and Peat had their attention trained on Hugh Jack, Nickie saw her opportunity and began running toward the Mercedes as fast as she could. Peat took off after her and caught up just as she reached the car. He tackled her and pinned her to the ground.

"Go on girl, fffight!" Peat said.

She pushed him off, kicking and slapping at him. She was able to meet her knee to his groin, and it slowed his urge enough to stop the attack. He stood with his hands on his knees doubled over in pain.

"Ggggget up bbbitch," Peat said as he placed a noose around her neck. "If you'll just chhhhhill, this will aaall…"

"Yeah, I get it," Nickie interrupted, impatient with the stuttering.

Peat walked Nickie back to the clearing. Hugh Jack stood with his hands over his head, tied to the two by eight. His cowboy hat had been knocked off, and he had a cut above his left eye. His round body stood stretched on his tiptoes, his face bleeding.

Turtle threw Peat a can of bug spray and he doused himself all over before turning to Nickie.

"We don't need this bbbbbeautiful bbbody of yours red and swwwollen with bbites," Peat said as he began dousing Nickie's body with bug spray.

"Well, go ahead and get started with your torture. Let's see how long I can last before I break and tell you everything you want to know."

"Oh, the torture's started. A soft city boy like you has no idea how bad the torture is for you right now. You're being tortured and don't even know it," Turtle said, smiling.

Hugh Jack stared at Turtle with hatred in his eyes. Hatred replacing his earlier fear. Hugh Jack hated rednecks, and Turtle McCowan was the epitome of a redneck. He hated the way he looked, tall and skinny, wearing faded Guess jeans with the ever-present Skoal can ring on the back pocket, Lynyrd Skynyrd t-shirt that clung tight to his undeveloped chest. His mullet, the feathered butt cut, supported a Mack Truck cap. The bill of the cap was rounded so much it was ineffective in keeping the sun from his eyes. The one thing Hugh Jack hated more than anything were his cheap Wal-Mart boots made of pleather.

It made him look like a wannabe cowboy, and Hugh Jack despised wannabes. But more than the appearance of Paul "Turtle" McCowan was the fact that he had control over Hugh Jack at the moment. Rarely did anyone or anything ever have control over him.

In his mind these boys were nothing more than white trash who lived in a trailer, born from a whore mother. They never really had a relationship with their father, the man they now confess their undying love and admiration for.

Hugh Jack looked confused. Turtle nor Peat made a move toward him.

"You're just going to sit there, what are we doing out here. We could have done this at the barn."

"Naw, we couldna done this at your barn," Turtle said.

Peat finished eating an apple and threw the core at Hugh Jack's feet, got up and grabbed some pruning shears. He disappeared in the woods and came back with a weed and a branch dangling from the shears.

Walking over to Hugh Jack, he held the two in front of him and asked him to identify what he saw.

"I don't know, are we out here for a damn botany lesson?"

"You'll neeeeeever forget these wwwwwwwwweeds after today," Peat laughed, laying the two weeds on the ground before him.

"This here is called pppoison ivy, the other one is pppoison oak. They both do about the same thing. You'll itch wherever it tttouches your ssskin. If you can't tttreat it or scratch it for a long tttime, it'll send you plumb crazy. I ain't heard of no one dying from it, but I'm sure you're going to wish you was."

Hugh Jack thought about the money. He had worked so

hard to rebuild the cash since his downfall. And the bones, he couldn't let these stupid rednecks get the bones. Those were worth another one hundred thousand dollars. *I can take a little itching.*

"So, you gonna tell us where the cash is," Turtle asked.

Hugh Jack stood, sweat pouring from him. Flies gathered around the apple core and flew into his face. Unable to shoo them away, he blew on them as they landed on his cheek just under his right eye. The constant blowing made him lightheaded, and he had to stop.

Turtle picked up the pruner and grabbed the poison oak, rubbing it under Hugh Jack's chin and all over his neck. Starting at each wrist, he rubbed it down each arm and into his arm pits, spending extra time there. He rubbed it all over his chest and down onto his stomach and stopped.

"Soap and water will stop the effects. Fifteen minutes. Right now, you have up to fifteen minutes to stop the poison oak from activatin'. Once it does, it can take from four to forty-eight hours for it to start itching and a rash to form. Now, if you choose not to take the soap and water, that's a shame because every minute you wait, these little bugs called chiggers are crawling up from the grass and weeds you're standing in and crawling all over your body. As a matter of fact, I'm not even going to rub this poison oak around your balls because the itch from the chiggers, or redbugs as some folks call them, is far worse than the poison oak."

Turtle appeared back at the clearing with a cooler. He took out a bottle of calamine lotion and showed it to Hugh Jack.

"Now this is what you'll need pretty soon. Usually in a couple of days, you'll start feeling the itch from the poison ivy. Calamine lotion is the only relief you can get. Of course, you soap up right now it should stop all this before it even gets started. I'll even let your little honey soap you up as a bonus."

"Screw you," Hugh Jack said, sending a stream of spit toward Turtle.

"Pppride goes before destruction, a hhhaughty spirit bbefore a fffall; that's from PPProverbs, my ddddamn mother used to say that to me over and over until one day I bbbeat the sssshit outta her," Peat said, anger showing on his face.

"That's a shame. See I was going to give your shriveled balls and ass a reprieve; but that disrespect just cost them an introduction to poison ivy," Turtle said as he walked behind Hugh Jack. He started at the top of his butt crack and ran it down, stopping just below the scrotum. He left the ivy in the crack of his rear and sat back down.

"We'll just wait and see how strong you are."

Turtle sat on the cooler and leaned against a tree. He cleaned his fingernails with his pocket knife and stared at Nickie.

"You gon' be covered in ticks soon. They itch too. I'll have Nickie here do a little inspection later and see if we can find any. They love dark hairy places, so I'm guessing you won't be using what the good Lord gave you anytime soon. Just tell your wife and girlfriend here you will be out of commission for a while."

"What kind of sick mind creates this kind of torture?" Hugh Jack said as a bead of sweat reached the tip of his nose, hanging there for an eternity, finally dropping to the ground.

Hugh Jack was unable to hold his bladder any longer. Letting go, it sprayed on the apple core at his feet, bouncing off of it and showering pearls all around him.

"Wwwell, you've ddddone it now. The ffflies gon' be all over you for sure."

Just as Peat said that, a fly landed on his forehead and crawled around his eyes. Hugh Jack blinked, shaking his head, but the flies just kept coming, more and more of them, darting at his face and landing on his chest. He could feel them all over him buzzing by his ear, like little kamikaze pilots darting in and out, flying all around his head, trying to end him.

"Oh, that just gave me a great idea!" Turtle said, as he reached into his cooler and brought out a jar of peanut butter. Unscrewing the cap, he scooped out a large amount and smeared it on Hugh Jack's forehead with a stick. Soon Hugh Jack stood in a cloud of flies buzzing around his head. They crawled into his nostrils. He felt them crawling in his ears.

Turtle moved the bottom of a plastic fifty-five-gallon barrel full of sloshing stagnate water just in front of Hugh Jack. Soon the slight buzzing of mosquitoes filled Hugh Jack's ear, causing him to jerk his head violently from side to side.

As he carefully observed, Turtle gave Hugh Jack a play by play of everything that was happening to him and everything that would happen.

Soon the mosquito bites began itching. Hugh Jack closed his eyes, trying to mentally escape the torture along with the quick spurts of buzzing and flies landing and walking all over his face and in his ears.

He closed his eyes and tried to settled himself. He slowly breathed in and out and focused his mind's eye on stacks of cash. The flies zapped in and out around his face and ears. The tiny buzz of mosquitos took residence in his ears. His eyes opened wildly and he and began thrusting, trying to break free from the tethers that bound him. The zip ties and rope cut deep into his skin, welcoming more bloodthirsty mosquitos.

"You are two sick bastards!" Hugh Jack whispered, his energy slowly being sucked from his body. The sun rising to its noon spot in the atmosphere now shone directly in his eyes. Sweat poured down his face, his skin slowly turning red.

The flies and mosquitoes increased in numbers, covering his body. A raven flew overhead and cawed. Hugh Jack shook and twisted again, moving as much as he could, trying to alleviate the pain and irritation.

He urinated again, and Turtle continued his play-by-play commentary. "Dehydration, that'll be next. As much as you're sweatin' and pissin', you'll be weak, sick, on top of itching to death. We're closing in on the fifth hour, the poison oak should kick in here shortly."

Hugh Jack cried out. Deep, guttural sounds emanating from him as he struggled to fight off the pain. His body tingling. A thousand places that needed to be scratched.

"Please take this branch out of my ass," Hugh Jack begged, writhing from discomfort.

A light tingling sensation formed just under his scrotum. He contorted his body into odd shapes as he tried to scratch the itch. With every movement, flies and mosquitos were jolted from their places on his body where they had chosen to feast. His armpits now showed signs of redness as they started itching. Red splotches broke out on his ankles and neck. He moved his head up and down trying to find relief. His rear now on fire. He tried moving toward the tree to rub it on the trunk, but he couldn't get close enough. Suspended between the trees, Hugh Jack found no way to scratch or move to eliminate the pain as it increased. His whole body felt as if he had been set on fire.

Thoughts of the money he had acquired swarmed in his head. He thought about regaining his ability to practice law and reopening his practice with the same locations as before. Images bounced in his head. Images of the bones, the women, all of the offices, he wanted his old life back. He wanted it all back, and in his mind, he was close. The bones were about to bring him in another load of cash. He was so close, and these redneck bastards were ruining it all.

Hugh Jack could no longer feel his arms. His shoulders burned. His wrists bled from his full weight pulling on the zip ties, all while mosquitos continued to feast.

He looked at Nickie, she was crying, trying to cover her nakedness.

His arm pits and crotch itched. Whelps formed on his neck. He hung, now all the weight on his wrists, swinging, unable to stand, his strength and energy zapped.

Peat stood from the stump where he sat and moved toward Nickie. She recoiled the closer he got. He slowly walked toward her like a lion stalking its prey. She turned as he got closer, and he grabbed the back of her neck, forcing his lips onto hers. Nickie pulled back, stumbled and fell. He sprang on top of her, his hands groping and kissing each inch of her body he could reach as she writhed on the ground. Nickie looked up at Hugh Jack, her eyes locked on his.

"I'll tell you!" he blurted out. "Leave her alone!"

All eyes focused on Hugh Jack.

"Take me down and we'll go back to the barn, I'll show you." Hugh Jack said, barely able to speak.

"Hhhow, do we know yyyou ain't lyin?" Peat said, looking at Turtle for agreement.

"You don't," Hugh Jack whispered, barely able to speak, his throat dry and parched.

"Looks like you've got a heart in there after all," Turtle said.

Peat moved toward Hugh Jack waving his hand as he did, shooing the flies and mosquitoes from their resting place. Careful where he stepped. He removed the poison ivy with the pruning shears. He cut the zip ties, and Hugh Jack fell to the ground. His shoulders slowly allowing his arms to lower. Finally able, he scratched his body, openly scratching his crotch, whimpering from the pain. His right arm stuck oddly from his side.

Nickie quickly dressed, then helped Hugh Jack to his feet. His body weak, she put his pants on him. She was only able to drape his shirt around his shoulders. She carried his boots and hat. She placed him in the passenger side of the car. Turtle took his place in the back seat, and she drove.

Hugh Jack continued scratching the large, red whelps all over his body. He scooted on the seat scratching his rear as best he could. His right arm of no use, he reached where he could with his left.

They arrived at the barn. Peat pulled in behind them in the Corvette, and along with Turtle, held them at gun point as they walked into the barn.

Nickie sat Hugh Jack on the bottom step of the stairs that led to the apartment.

"I know where the money is," she whispered to him.

He gave her a sideways glance unsure of her plan. *No way can she know where the money is hidden.* He stopped thinking and started scratching. All of a sudden, he no longer cared about the money. His body contorted in pain. He couldn't reach all of the places that needed to be scratched.

"Lllet's go, where ii..." Peat tried to speak before Nickie interrupted him again, waving them toward the tack room.

She removed the hay bales and went through the same process as before to open the hidden door. As soon as it opened, she grabbed the shotgun from just inside the door and pointed it at Turtle and Peat.

Turtle immediately lunged toward her, and she pulled the trigger, but nothing happened. He grabbed the gun from her and backhanded her, sending her to the floor. He broke open the double barrel. It wasn't loaded.

"Why the hell would you have this money here and a gun that ain't loaded!" Nickie shouted at Hugh Jack.

"Guns don't work unless you load them!"

"Yeah, ggguns do..."

"Shut up you stutterin' bastard," Nickie shouted at Peat, her patience finished with him.

Turtle and Peat grabbed the bags of money and the leather suitcase. As they ran out of the barn, they thanked Hugh Jack as they passed him. They loaded the Corvette and fishtailed onto the road, kicking up rocks and mud as they left.

Night

Blackness forms from shut eyes. A room slowly comes into view. A small portion at first, then finally showing itself fully. Two chairs facing each other. A small coffee table dividing them, holding a note pad and pen in its center, lined neatly. The room was round. Dark mahogany encircles the chairs. A grand piano near a window softly and slowly playing in minor keys.

The synapses in his brain dull and tired. A light shining turning the room stark white. His dreams, the title of books, lining the room surrounding him. In order from earliest memory to the most recent. A childhood that wouldn't leave him alone. Dreams of his father filling his darkest corners.

Tell me about the last dream you had, the therapist says. She sits rigid in a straight-backed chair writing, taking blank notes, expressionless, asking questions, and prodding to tell her more. Her face a skull covered in skin. Her eyes missing, her mouth speaking.

The darkness of an attic. Tell me the story, she says. Two figures hiding, trying to stay away from what was coming. Headlights in a driveway, two people scurrying into an attic, pulling the stairs up behind them, sitting and waiting in the dark. The sweltering heat zapping energy; sweat pouring, flooding their faces. Doors slamming open, sounds of splintering wood and metal clashing. Guttural screams filling the quiet. Heavy Crying, calling their names. Russ, Jaimey. Calling over and over. Breaking glass, slamming doors, calling our names. Russ, Jaimey. The night goes silent. Attic stairs suddenly jerked down. The blackness of the attic suddenly introduced to light. A dark form ascending the stairs so quickly, grabbing us, pulling us down. Both on the floor, defending blows, lying beside each other, blocking the beating.

Large strong dark hands reaching our throat, squeezing tighter and tighter until the light fades to black. Falling through the darkness, unable to stop. The blackness slowly leaves. Waking breathless. The hand is gone. Morning light shines bright again. His fixed eyes stare back at me.

CHAPTER THIRTEEN

"Before we drive by the warehouse, let's find out where Hugh Jack is," Bubba said, as he pointed his car toward Hugh Jack's house.

He made a slow pass by his house and saw Hugh Jack's truck parked in the yard. The next stop was the law office. His wife's car was there, but no sign of Hugh Jack's Mercedes. He arrived at the barn and slowed as he made the curve and saw the Mercedes.

He reached the bypass and gunned it but immediately slowed when he saw the flashing lights of a patrol car ahead. He passed them at the proper speed, but floored it again as the patrol car dropped out of sight. Bubba pulled into the street that ran beside the warehouse and parked behind it. They walked to the side door on the addition and noticed a pane of glass had been broken and the door was unlocked.

"You're right, he could park inside here," Russ said, as he and Bubba made their way upstairs.

They reached the second floor and noticed the platforms with the pulley system.

"He'll be up here waiting when I arrive. When he knows I'm here, he'll place the remains on the platform. I'll place the bag of money on the platform downstairs. He'll work the pulley system, and the exchange will be made. He'll be downstairs and, in his car, as fast as his fat ass will let him. He'll be out of the door and gone," Russ said.

As Russ talked the plan through, he walked it as well, rehearsing the steps. They made their way back downstairs.

"While he's upstairs, you can slip in the back of his car and be waiting. We'll stop him, get our money back. We've got the remains, we'll be golden."

They left the warehouse and made their way up the street that eventually made a horseshoe turn around three houses that bordered another street behind it. They turned back onto Main Street.

They took main street back to the office. They returned to the conference room, planning, plotting, putting final touches on who would be where and when, and what Bubba would do when Hugh Jack finally got back into the truck. They considered using guns, but this was Hugh Jack they were dealing with. He was harmless ... a slow fat cat with a cowboy hat, boots, and expensive jewelry. He hadn't broken a sweat in years, unless it was in the bedroom.

CHAPTER FOURTEEN

Hugh Jack lay nude on the bed, covered in calamine lotion. He lay on his stomach with his rear poked in the air and his cheeks spread apart trying to get relief, the ceiling fan on high above him. When his front side became too uncomfortable to lay on, he turned on his back and lay on his sides, switching, trying to find comfort, rubbing the calamine lotion off every time he moved.

As he switched again onto his stomach, he called Nickie to rub more lotion on the parts he couldn't reach.

"I've seen you naked already. I don't know why I have to leave every time you turn over."

He called his wife to tell her he had to run out of town last minute to finalize some old cases. She wouldn't expect him home for a week. The doctor had been called and would make a house call at lunch with shots, medication, and salve for the various bites and rashes.

"I had a damn plan," Hugh Jack blurted out, his mind unable to let go of the recent events.

"Who the hell has a gun that ain't loaded near a fortune?" Nickie asked.

"Oh, here we go again!"

"If that damn gun was loaded you wouldn't have lost your money or your damn bones," Nickie said...again.

"And I 'spose you would have shot them both?"

Nickie didn't answer.

"I need you to go to my car and look under the passenger seat and bring me the black book you'll find under there."

"I ain't your damn secretary," Nickie said.

"I'll pay you, please."

"With what? You ain't got no damn money," Nickie said, laughing as she left to go to the car. "He even took the six hundred dollars in your damn wallet."

She returned with the book and handed it to Hugh Jack who was now propped on his side, waiting for it, a towel draped over his crotch. He sat up and scratched his legs. The relief was only temporary. The scratching made the pain worse. His body was a mixture of white, red, and pink. Thick lines of blood formed from scratching mixed with the calamine lotion created a strange light red hue.

"You almost look like a damn candy cane," she said through a slight laugh.

"Where in the hell is that doctor? Get his ass here," Hugh Jack said as he thrust himself around on the bed, trying to find comfort in a new position.

"Hey, I know you're in pain, but don't holler at me, and don't tell me what to do."

"Sorry, this is just unbearable," Hugh Jack said, flipping through his book.

He sat up and scratched his legs again. "The calamine

lotion helps with the poison oak and poison ivy, but the chigger bites are the worst," Hugh Jack said.

With both hands he scratched wildly all over his head and neck where the mosquitos concentrated their efforts. Between his head, neck, and legs he scratched and they bled.

"Please turn that ceiling fan on higher," Hugh Jack said. "That air helps a little."

"Would you step outside and give me a little privacy? Actually, would you go to the store and get another bottle of calamine lotion?"

"Sure. You hungry?"

"Yeah, get us whatever you want." Hugh Jack said as he reached between the mattress and box spring and pulled out a small stack of twenties. "Keep the change, payment for putting up with me."

After he heard the door to the outside close, he dialed a number from his book.

"Red, I have a job for you. You up for it?" Hugh Jack asked.

"Well, I guess it de..."

"Hey... Hey Red, hold on a minute," Hugh Jack put the phone down while he scratched himself. He jumped down from the bed and scooted his ass on the carpet like a dog. Tears fell in large chunks from his eyes.

"Sorry about that, got into a bunch of chiggers yesterday, itching like crazy," he said almost out of breath.

"Nothing worse that chiggers," Red agreed, showing a rare amount of compassion. "What do you need Hugh, and how are you gonna pay me?"

"I need you to dig up a set of bones, not a cadaver. I need bones, old bones."

"What in the hell do you need with bones, you mean a skeleton?" Red asked, unbelieving.

"It's better you don't know. I've got the money. What's it going to take?"

"Grave robing, this'll be a first for me … quite a bit of risk, not to mention the work of digging up a grave. I'll need some help."

"Get your brother. I trust him to keep quiet, but would be better if he didn't know this was for me. Hang on," Hugh Jack said as he put the phone down again and scratched. He walked over to the freezer and pulled the wet towel that was cooling and walked back to the phone. He took each end of the cold towel and straddled it pulling it between his cheeks and sat down. He let out a sigh of relief.

"Okay Red I'm back."

"Five thousand," Red said. "When do you need them?"

"End of the week. These bones need to be about fifteen plus years old, hear?"

"Yeah. Okay, I'll pull one from a grave with year of death in the eighties. Will that work?"

"That should work. I'll be at my barn, but call before you show up, okay. I've got a little honey out here."

"Wouldn't be Hugh Jack Rives unless you did," Red said. "Is that where the chiggers came from, screwing outdoors?"

"That would be a better story than the real one. Thanks, Red."

CHAPTER FIFTEEN

Darrell "Red" O'Halloran walked through the Masonic cemetery gate shining a flashlight, bouncing from one grave stone to another. The dates on most dated back to the late 1800's, early 1900's. The cemetery was the first one in Lewiston.

Red stood in a grove of hundred plus year old oaks. He stared through the canopy of gnarled limbs into the clear dark sky peppered with stars. He walked through the grove shining the stones. The ones he couldn't read he didn't consider. Most of the markers under the oaks were mildewed and weathered, telling of their age.

He came across one from 1978, Korea and Viet Nam were listed under the soldier's name and he refused to disturb the grave.

He moved toward the end of the graveyard where newer trees had been planted hoping more recent tombstones would be as well. His hunch was right. He needed one from the late seventies, early eighties. His experience told him an embalmed body needs at least fifteen years to decompose.

Red looked around the darkened cemetery and then

stared back at the tombstone. He read the name and re-read the dates just to be certain.

"This should do. Charlie, go get the excavator. Let's dig this one up," Red said.

As Red waited for Charlie and stared at the tombstone he couldn't remember if Hugh Jack said he need Male or female bones. He read the tombstone again.

William Brian Russell
Beloved Husband and Son
1956-1979

"Hell, it couldn't make that much difference, Hugh just needed bones, so bones are what he'll get." Red mumbled out loud to himself.

Red watched, looked around again as he heard Charlie start the excavator and back it off the trailer. Watching for anyone who might be suspicious of their activity. Watching the highway for the sudden red lights of a braking car. Thankful the cemetery was out in the country.

Charlie returned with the excavator and began digging. It didn't take long before they were scraping the top of the casket.

"Hey, what the hell you think you're doing out here in the middle of the night," a slight older man asked as he stood weaving before them unsteady on his feet, waving a bottle of Gin in the air, pointing toward the grave.

Red pulled a revolver with a silencer from his waist and placed a bullet in the man's head.

Charlie jumped down into the grave and removed the remainder of the dirt, scraping it off of the top of the casket with a shovel. He opened the casket and just as Red hoped, only bones lay before them. Red placed a large suitcase beside the grave, and Charlie gingerly took out the skeleton out by sections. He left the casket open and rolled the drunk along with his bottle into the casket and closed it. They replaced the dirt, packed it down, quickly resodded the top with the grass they scraped off, scattered some leaves around it, loaded the excavator and left.

Night

A small dot of brilliant white centered in a bright green surrounded by darkness appeared. The light grew in circumference. A dark vertical strip in its center, growing taller, soon took over the light. The vertical strip slowly began walking, gaining ground, emanating a green glow. The strip soon grew arms and a face, a maddening face showing no peace or joy. Its face and mouth screamed, but no sound. A long finger pointed, the tip now taking up his complete vision, pointed as if to blame, as if saying it's all your fault. Then the finger zoomed off, returning, curled, joining a fist, hitting and grabbing and drinking. The lips and teeth, now visible, formed curse words ... in silence screaming blame and hatred from the vision that now showed a face. The face of a father without love, dark and now blank, lost flesh; fresh with dirt, empty eyes, black sockets.

Breathing turning toward hyperventilation as he woke. He reached toward the light as his eyes opened. Reaching toward the light, and the green, and the man. Reaching to choke him, trying to kill him, trying to kill the dream. Trying to kill the flashes of the man who simply wouldn't die.

CHAPTER SIXTEEN

The following morning Red called Hugh Jack at the barn. Hugh Jack lay in the tub, rubbing his parts that itched the worst, unable to scratch and unwilling to give blood any longer. He added Epsom salt to the hot water, swirling it around the tub, allowing it to cover every inch of his body that wretched in pain. The salt sifted through the water and lay in the open sores slightly burning, feeling as if they were cauterizing the torn flesh. It gave him relief.

The steroid shot his doctor had given him the previous day helped with the poison oak and ivy, but the chigger bites, the damn chigger bites made him feel as if he would go insane from the itching. He considered staying in the tub all day, the only place where relief was found, but he had business to take care of.

"I've got it, where should we meet?" Red asked, anxious to retrieve the cash.

"The motor home at the lake. Let's wait till dark around 8:00. Be on time. This has got to be quick. I'll need to get back here. This itching is driving me crazy."

CHAPTER SEVENTEEN

Nickie ran into Huny and Bandit at the store just down from the barn where she had first met them.

"Where y'all two been, church?" Nickie asked, shocked at how well they cleaned up.

"We been at a singin'. We sing at funerals, the Apostolic church on Sundays, sometimes weddings. Well, I sing, Bandit plays the guitar," Huny said as she lit a Swisher Sweet cigarillo and blew it away from Nickie.

As Nickie walked through the store, she filled a hand-held basket with various items while Huny followed her and talked. Nickie still unsure if she could trust the two of them.

"Where do you live, hun?"

"Different places. I kinda move around a lot," Nickie said, suddenly feeling the desperate longing for a real family. She missed her mother and father. Her mind started going down into the long, dark rabbit hole where it sometimes headed, thinking about how screwed up her life had become. She felt herself slipping into her old routine of going over every single bad thing that ever happened to her, only to be interrupted by Bandit's voice.

"We going to smoke some weed, wanna come?" Bandit asked, his eyes bright and happy.

"I ain't got mine."

"I got you covered," Huny said as she put her arm around Nickie, giving her a quick squeeze. Nickie smiled at the comfort Huny provided.

She paid for the few items she had and crawled into the van with Bandit and Huny. They drove toward the same resort where Bandit sold the hippies the weed before. The last of the sun falling behind the lake as they crested the hill. The street lights, and the exterior lights on the restaurant, popped on as they drove past. Bandit took the same turn beside the same motel on the same gravel road that led to the same motor homes and pull-behind trailers and parked at the same trailer the hippies lived in.

"This where we goin' to smoke, with these two hippies?"

"Yeah baby, they're friends of ours, best people you'll ever meet," Huny said, as she extinguished her Swisher Sweet in a tree stump beside where they parked.

Nickie followed Bandit and Huny into the trailer and was immediately greeted with hugs from the two hippies. As they hugged her, they both smelled like a mixture of pot, body odor, and fruity incense.

The woman was the second to greet her, and Nickie noticed she still hadn't shaved her arm pits. Luckily, today she was wearing a tank top. She was high and held onto the hug a little too long, making Nickie feel uncomfortable.

"This is Lennon and Caledonia," Huny said as she made introductions.

Lennon handed Nickie her own joint and lit it. The light

murmur of conversation hung in the air like the thick smoke that hovered over them. As she looked around the small twenty-foot travel trailer, a strange feeling of familiarity overtook her as she watched Lennon light everyone's joint.

A Jimi Hendrix poster was taped on the wall with scotch tape, layered with psychedelic images over a portion of it. Playing low on a stereo was Janis Joplin followed by The Moody Blues. A record collection leaned sideways in a milk crate, and she flipped through them—Carol King, The Grateful Dead, Bob Dylan, James Taylor. Her parents had many of the same albums, and she started down the rabbit hole again.

She was jolted from her descent by Caledonia as she asked if she knew many of the artists on the albums.

"My folks had a lot of the same ones," she said.

Caledonia took Nickie by the hand and brought her over to complete the circle they all sat in. By this time Lennon and Bandit had finished their roaches and Lennon passed around a bong. It reached Nickie and she breathed in the smoke, while Lennon held a lighter to the stem. The bubbling, gurgling noise filled the air and took over the now quiet atmosphere as they all sat in a circle stoned, numb and unfeeling.

Nickie felt a hand take hers and raise it above her head as Jerry Garcia sang "Scarlet Begonias." Caledonia danced while sitting, her head hanging low, pumping her arms in the air and keeping rhythm with Bob Weir's guitar.

"You ever dropped acid?" Caledonia asked.

Nickie simply shook her head.

Huny got up as fast as the pot would allow her and grabbed Nickie's hand to pull her out of the trailer and away from the situation, now regretting bringing the young girl into the mess, but Nickie pulled her hand away.

Caledonia held a small square piece of paper with a dancing bear on it.

"Stick out your tongue," she said, as she stuck out her own, demonstrating for Nickie how to take the acid.

Nickie leaned her head back slightly and stuck out her tongue. Caledonia placed the small stamp with the dancing bear on the tip.

"Now close your mouth and eyes and wait," Caledonia said as she placed one on her tongue as well.

Nickie sat for a long while before feeling slightly dizzy. She soon stood and moved around the trailer, looking at everything as if it was new. She reached out, touching the air around her. She stood in front of the Jimi Hendrix poster for close to an hour staring at the colors again, trying to touch them, following them as they moved. She walked across the room as if she were following something, as if she were chasing it. With her hands held in front of her she touched the walls and eventually found the door.

Lennon walked with her as she made her way outside.

"She's finally seeing things for what they really are," he said to no one in particular. "The trees, yes the bark," Lennon said, as if he were giving Nickie her own guided tour of the forest as it appears on acid.

They walked outside for hours just feet from the front door, inspecting blades of grass, sifting handfuls of dried dirt, and flaking pieces of pine bark from trees. Nickie stood still for several minutes watching the vibration of the antennae on Bandit's van as she flicked her finger on it, over and over, moving it back and forth.

"Yes, feel the vibration," Lennon said.

Caledonia walked around the trailer park inspecting the

siding on the other trailers, looking inside their windows, and dancing to the silent music in her head.

After a couple of hours, the affects began to ease, and Nickie had to use the bathroom. She sat on the commode and watched as a car's headlights shone in the window. She freaked out as the light appeared as if it would come right into the bathroom.

A man with red hair got out of the car and opened the rear door, reached in and retrieved a large suitcase, very similar to the one stored in Hugh Jack's secret hiding place.

She finished using the bathroom and cleaned herself and stood, continuing to watch, wondering if what she saw was real.

The man came out of the trailer with a smaller bag and got in his car and sped off, his tail lights dancing as the tires rolled over the rough road. As he left, all of the lights in the trailer began turning off, and a large, dark figure holding a large, dark suitcase walked out of the door, stopping long enough to lock the door behind him. He scratched under his chin and the back of his neck.

"Hugh Jack?" Nickie questioned herself, she couldn't be sure of what she was witnessing, her brain having just processed the vibration of an antennae.

The large man popped the trunk, placed the suitcase in the back, and plopped down in the driver's seat, the car rocking with his weight. As he cranked the car, the interior glow illuminated Hugh Jack's round face and cowboy hat. The red glow from a cigar illuminated his eyes again, and the car filled with smoke. Nickie made out his two class rings on each hand. She saw him scratch under his chin again.

That's Hugh Jack. She could barely process what she had just seen.

Her silent spotting of the fat man in the wild was interrupted by a slight knock on her door. She moved toward the door and opened it. A young girl stood in front of her looking as if she had just awakened from a deep sleep. Her hair was greasy, wild and matted, as if it had not been brushed in days. She was dressed in a plaid school uniform, holding herself.

"I need to use the bathroom."

Without saying anything, Nickie stepped outside and closed the door behind her. She collapsed. Her back hit the wall and she slid down, sitting now with her head buried in her hands resting on her knees. Her senses dulled and slowly she began weeping, then stood and screamed.

"Nooooooo!"

She ran down the hall and stood in front of the door. She stared at Lennon. His long hair and beard and creepy stupid smile made her sick to her stomach, and she turned and vomited out the door. She turned and saw a man standing where Lennon stood; long beard, dirty t-shirt covered in crusted food and stained with fast food condiments. He was nude from the waist down.

She moved frantically. Her hands and eyes tracing unreal images in the air. Everyone watching her as she bounced from wall to wall as if she were trying to escape from the room.

As Huny moved toward her, Nickie screamed, "No!" and pushed her away.

The trailer soon took on another shape, smaller, dirtier. Nude pictures of women hung on the wall. Crushed beer cans and whiskey bottles lay everywhere. Food containers and their contents littered the floor and the kitchen counters. The smell of human waste and body odor suddenly permeated Nickie's nose. She stood in the doorway crying, out of her mind, seeing nothing in the present and everything from her past. Her parent's funeral, their wrecked SUV, crinkled like a candy wrapper, the foster homes, the damn foster homes, where she was abused over and over again. No one ever believed her. The mall and grocery store the day she first saw Danny "Crabs" Williams. It all came flooding back. Her brain was on fire, and she wanted to put it out. She turned and ran toward the lake and down the long pier, picking up speed as she did, and jumped and let herself fall limp from the pier. Her eyes opened under water, unafraid of dying, staring up into the dark night splattered with dots of lights blinking on and off. Her mind swarmed with memories of pot, acid, and all the shit people had told her and done to her all of her life.

Her vision made out a slow, heavy form on the end of the pier, then others appeared as the first jumped in the water. Nickie's arms and hands flailing, Huny jerked her out of the water, and Bandit reached down and pulled her up and laid her out on the pier, rolling her onto her side and pumping her stomach. She coughed and spit water from her mouth and started fighting him. Huny rushed to her side and held her, stroking her hair until the morning sun began to rise.

CHAPTER EIGHTEEN

Only one week was left before the planned exchange took place. The pain and agony Hugh Jack had been suffering was still present, but had subsided. With ChiggerX and calamine lotion, he was able to better tolerate the itching.

He guessed that Nickie had finally had enough and moved on, even though she had left a few things in the apartment. He looked through her bag, thinking she may have taken some money and was surprised when he didn't find any.

He was locked in the tack room cleaning the bones that Red had acquired. He positioned the skeleton much as he had when he first discovered his remains. As he worked with them, he noticed the remains were shorter than Randy Crawford's.

I guess there's no way you can determine height just by looking at a tombstone.

He had placed the last piece of the skeleton in the suitcase and closed the clasps on each end when he heard the barn door open. He grabbed his thirty-eight from his waist and quickly placed the suitcase in its hiding place. He reached his hand down inside his pants and scratched his crotch again. He considered for a moment changing hiding places for these bones, but the last time anyone saw his secret room it was empty, so no one would suspect anything hidden there.

He was anxious to get the other bones and money back from Turtle and Peat, but that would take money, and Red would require more than five grand to do that job. He was suspicious of Red as a rule.

Red might just help himself to the money, kill the McCowan brothers to cover his tracks, and disappear.

The door to the apartment closed, and he figured Nickie had returned from whatever she had been doing the night before. He heard what sounded like her plopping on the bed, which squeaked every time someone moved on it.

He quietly pushed the suitcase all the way to the back of the wall, trying to conceal it as much as he could, and replaced the hay around the secret opening just as it was before everything was stolen.

Nickie lay on the bed and heard movement below her and wondered what Hugh Jack was doing in there this time. She made a mental note to check it out later as she quickly fell asleep.

The itching never stopped. Hugh Jack hurried up to the apartment. It was time for more lotion and medicine and another soak in the Epsom salt. The nearer he got, soaking in a hot Epsom salt bath felt like the only thing that would provide relief.

He opened the door and saw Nickie lying nude on her stomach on the bed. She lie diagonally across the bed and had not moved since she plopped down. She looked dirty and smelled bad like strange tobacco. He took a blanket and covered her and put a pillow under her head and hoped and prayed his wife didn't show up.

Hugh Jack drew a hot tub full of water, added the Epsom salt, and eased himself in. It took a while because the water was hot, but he was finally able to submerge himself up to his neck and felt instant relief. He applied calamine lotion to the places on his face and behind his ears where the chiggers had found hiding spots and attached themselves.

He soaked for as long as he could until the water started cooling. He had been lying in the tub thinking of what he would tell number four. He needed to go home today. His "trip" was finally over. He couldn't stay away any longer. How in the hell would he explain the bites all over his body and the itching? Most of all, how would he explain the fact that he didn't want to have sex when he got home. He always needed sex when he had been away, and now he simply didn't feel like it. Of all things, that is what would make her the most suspicious. *I may just have to grit my teeth and do it.*

He soaked in the warm water and concocted a fishing story that would explain the bites and poison ivy. Hugh Jack got out of the tub, dried off, got dressed, left a hundred dollars and a note by the bed for Nickie and went home.

CHAPTER NINETEEN

The suitcase was the first bag that Turtle and Peat opened when they got back to the compound. It was the largest so they thought it would have the most money in it.

"Son of a bitch," Turtle said as he recoiled, unwrapping the bones from the towels. "What the hell has Hugh Jack done?"

"Shit, this is even too mmmmuch for Hugh Jack. I never ssssspotted him a killer, you?" Peat asked, holding back a towel and peering into the suitcase. "This is Hugh Jack's suitcase ffffor sure, probably had it made to match a pair of bbboots."

"No shit, that bastard loves to get dressed up, don't he?" Turtle said.

"Wwwwhat in the hhhell are we gonna ddo with these?"

"We'll figure something. Check out the others," Turtle said, grabbing a duffle bag.

They each slowly opened a bag, peeking into them, unsure of what they would see. A sea of green lay before them. Every denomination, mostly fifties on top, some flat stacks, some rolls.

Turtle and Peat started celebrating, opening the other bags, running their hands down among the cash.

"WWe got to ccccount all this to see how much it is," Peat said, as he held a fat roll of cash.

"Hell, Peat, you know how long it would take you to count one of these bags. Good lord, we never would get through."

"You ssson-of-a-bbbitch. I might tttalk slow, but I can ccount fffast, I'll sing the numbers if I have to."

"Look, we've got to hide this and keep it hid. We need to bury it so it can't be found. You go dig us a hole while I start countin'. Make it long and deep enough to put this suitcase in it, too, till we figure things out. Go dig back by the lake."

"Ssscrew you, Tturtle."

"Go on now."

Turtle took all the bags inside the house and cleaned off a spot on the floor. From the den ceiling hung drying turtle shells, and he had to duck as he entered the room.

As he brushed by them, they moved in the wind, sounding like wind chimes as they clanked together. He had been meaning to add wind chimes to his list of things to make from the shells. He placed the bags on top of each other and divided the denominations into separate stacks and started counting.

It took him three hours to count the first bag. Turtle had never seen this much money before. He started thinking about what he could do with this kind of cash, where he could go, what kind of car he could buy, and how many women he could start dating.

"The good ones too, not some cheap, white trailer trash slut neither," he said out loud to himself.

He thought about a new car and what kind he wanted.

A new 'vette, and a new truck ... and some new clothes, some fancy clothes.

Each bag held a lot of loose bills. The rolls and stacks of larger denominations sat on top of the loose bills. There was plenty of money but not as much as it first appeared.

Turtle stood carefully, ducking under the hanging turtle shells, and looked out the window. He saw Peat from the waist up in the hole he was digging. Three hours into the work, Peat had made the hole much larger than was needed.

He looked back toward the duffle bags full of money, and his mind traveled to Florida. He had never been and always wanted to go. Then pictures of Alaska popped in his mind, another place he had always wanted to visit. He had been stuck in Lewiston his entire life, taking care of a brother who could barely talk and depended on him every second of the day. Turtle considered how many times his life was interrupted because Peat had to ask him some stupid question that meant nothing. Not to mention that his patience was done from having to wait until Peat got the words out. Peat had always been right up under Turtle. Step for step he had always been right there. His mother pawned Peat off on Turtle when they were teenagers and he had basically raised Peat from childhood.

"I've never had my own life," Turtle said out loud. "He's always been right there by my side since the day he was born. I shouldn't be burdened with this. He's not my responsibility. Now I've got the opportunity to finally go to all the places I've always wanted to go and I'm still trapped. I've got to get out of here before Hugh Jack is able to find me."

He walked toward the pond where Peat was now,

almost up to his chest throwing out dirt one shovel full after the other. The dirt pile grew by the minute.

He won't stop until I tell him to, dumb bastard.

Peat stopped his work and propped himself on the shovel staring at Turtle with a smile on his face.

"Wwwhat are you ddoing?"

Turtle stood twenty yards from Peat with his bow at full draw and released an arrow into Peat's chest. His smile turned to a pained shock, and blood oozed from the corner of his mouth as he stared down at the arrow sticking out of his chest. He sucked in air as he tried to breath, leaning heavy on the shovel's handle. His body slowly sank into the grave he just dug. Turtle walked to the hole. Peat lay propped on his elbow, the other hand still gripping the shovel. His eyes looked up at Turtle, asking why. He couldn't speak. Then his body relaxed, his hand slipped from the shovel. His gaze was steady and locked now staring straight into the side of his final resting place.

Turtle took the shovel and filled the hole. He was free. It was time for him to go.

CHAPTER TWENTY

Nickie woke to the smell of wet dog and the distant sound of men laughing and hollering. She heard it before. The barn was surrounded by a golf course, and it was Saturday morning. The entire day would be filled with noise.

She rose and went to the bathroom where she sat, rubbing her eyes. She popped an unlit cigarette in her mouth, wishing she could light it. Her mind burned with the memory of the previous night. The acid was something she never wanted to try a second time. The memories it dug up that she had pushed back into the far recesses of her mind never needed to show themselves again. She had worked hard to try and forget about her childhood, and up until now, she had been successful.

"Dammit!"

She hit her forehead with the palm of her hand as if pounding the previous night away.

"That damn trailer, that damn little girl!"

And then she stopped.

Who was the little girl? Were the hippies her real mom and dad or were they holding her there?

Nickie's imagination ran away with her. She jumped up, quickly got dressed, and ran all the way to the store. Huny and Bandit were in their usual spots by the pot belly stove eating Nabs and drinking Cokes.

Huny stood and met Nickie as she came in.

"You okay, hun?"

"The little girl, was that Lennon and Caledonia's little girl?"

"No. What little girl? They ain't got no little girl," Huny said, a confused look on her face.

"I saw a little girl when I was using the bathroom last night."

"There wadn't no little girl there, they was only us and Lennon and Caledonia," Bandit said. "Damn, you were trippin'."

"You, okay?" asked Huny. "They shouldn't have give you that acid. That'll make you do some strange shit, see some weird things."

"Make you relive your past," Nickie said, as she turned and left the store.

"Yep, make you do that, too," Huny answered, her voice trailing off as Nickie closed the door behind her.

He first heard laughing ... a maniacal laugh that sounded familiar. It kept rising and falling, up and down like a kid jumping on a pogo stick. He saw nothing, just heard the laughing. It was the same laughter his father had when he was proud of himself for inflicting abuse of some sort on either him or his mother. Up and down, it continued, and then he saw it. He was suddenly in the warehouse, standing, hovering in midair in front of the platforms being raised and lowered by Hugh Jack as he sang "Cathy's Clown" by the Everly Brothers. A dollar sign appeared on one platform, and as it disappeared, a dancing skeleton came into view on the other. A white dancing skeleton surrounded by dark. With each pass the dollar sign kept decreasing in size while the skeleton increased. The skeleton took on the flesh and blood form of his father, and he stood with a golf club in his hand leaning on it, smiling. Soon he began heaving, and then vomiting. Cash, in every denomination, flowed from his mouth.

"Satisfied? How's your life now, boy?" The skeleton returned, speaking.

Russ woke sweating, haunted.

CHAPTER TWENTY-ONE

ugh Jack, along with a small group of members, formed Smyth Creek Methodist Church. They built it from the ground up. Small on purpose. He attended services faithfully, rarely missing a Sunday since the late seventies. Teaching Sunday School fit Hugh Jack. His deep, rich voice lectured, taking on the tenor of a preacher when speaking. Scripture flowing from the King James Version from memory as he taught.

Hugh Jack owned every room he walked into. His understanding of theatrics in the court room paid dividends in the Sunday school room as well. He spoke with authority. At times he whispered so low the members had to lean in to hear him. He kept them spellbound and in the palm of his hand bringing stories to life straight from the Bible.

He often gestured with his hands as he spoke, his Rolex watch and chain bracelet falling just beyond the cuffs of his suit coat. In the summer, to the delight of his female students, his skin tanned darker against his white hair. His white teeth showing through his constant flirtatious smile.

His hat glided off his head timed perfectly as his foot crossed the threshold of the church's front door speaking to the women waiting on him to arrive. Greeting them with a slight bow. Complimenting their recent trips to the hair dresser and their new dresses they had purchased just for him. Asking about their children and grandchildren by name. He always showed an interest in their families. Remembering their children's ages and where they attended school.

His boots always shined, his pants had a crease in them that could cut butter, and his heavily starched shirt buttons were lined up straight with his fly. He constantly fooled with his tie, smoothing it and keeping it lined with his belt buckle.

He and his wife attended their respective churches after they married. It made swooning from the church widows much easier since she was never there. Hugh Jack was free to be his usual jovial self.

Today he taught the lesson of the woman at the well. He, wondered how many of these fine Christians would still feel the same about him, if they knew he stood strung up naked in front of a twenty-two-year-old girl just over a week ago. He wondered what they would think if they knew he had been tortured to gain knowledge of where money that he had stolen was located. Or that he had that same twenty-two-year-old girl living in his apartment right now, probably walking around half dressed. Or that he just paid a mobster five thousand dollars to rob a grave just days earlier. The list went on and on.

Hugh Jack had tried to get Nickie to attend Sunday services with him, not considering the avalanche of gossip that would follow. He purchased her a new dress, knowing all the while she would never attend.

She remained at the barn. Sitting on the deck of the apartment, looking out over the golf course, smoking a cigarette to calm her nerves. She was scared the little girl would return. That would be the last time she dropped acid, that much she knew for sure. Maybe that would keep the ghosts away.

Still, it was gnawing at her, stuck in the pit of her stomach. Ashes fell as her right leg bounced. Nervous energy brought her free hand near her mouth as she tried evening up her nails she had already trimmed with her teeth.

She finished her cigarette and flicked it onto the ground below, not caring if Hugh Jack saw it or not. Her mind trailed off as she thought about what Hugh Jack was doing below the stairs last night.

She closed the French doors and locked them and made her way down to the tack room. She pulled a bobby pin from her hair and opened the lock. She removed the hay bales and stepped on the board, lifted it, reached down inside the floor, pulled the ring, and just as happened last time, the door opened.

Inside was a large suitcase very similar to the other one. Beside it was a different shotgun. She broke open the two barrels and smiled as she noticed it was loaded. She replaced the gun and slid the suitcase out and unzipped it. She opened it and stared at clean white towels which she thought was strange. Unnerved, she pulled a corner back and recoiled. She fell back on her rear, catching herself, leaning on her hands, and scrambling to get away from the suitcase with her feet moving although never catching traction.

She continued staring at what showed of the contents, half a human skull staring back at her. She stood, shaking her hands as if she had touched something vile. She didn't want to touch it again, or even get anywhere near it for that matter.

Her mind began doing backflips wondering where it came from.

Had Hugh Jack somehow gotten the money and this suitcase back from Turtle and Peat? Did he kill the person who is in the suitcase? What had he done to the men who took it? Is he a murderer? Where's the money?

"Dammit girl, what in the hell are you doing?" Hugh Jack asked as he suddenly filled the doorway.

"Stay away from me, you crazy bastard," Nickie said backing away from Hugh Jack further from the door toward the back wall.

"Hell, Darlin.' I ain't goin' to hurt you," Hugh Jack said as he bent down to zip up the suitcase and slide it back into its hiding place.

"Who the hell is that?"

"To be honest, I have not got a damn clue."

"Did you kill that man, or woman, or whatever it is?"

"No, I didn't, I've never killed anybody in my life, it's a long story. Do you want to hear it? I've got to have a drink anyway."

Nickie stared at Hugh Jack for a long time, contemplating whether she should trust him or not. She stood with her arms folded tightly against her. She had still not fully recovered from her night spent on acid and almost drowning.

"I guess, but I don't want nothin' to drink."

Hugh Jack filled a tumbler with ice and filled it halfway with George Dickel. He forcefully shook in some bitters squeezed in a couple of orange slices, added some cherry juice and two cherries, stirred it once for good measure and walked up the stairs through the French doors and sat on an Adirondack chair, squeezing his midsection between the arm rests.

"Hell, I'll never be able to get out of here. Damn," Hugh Jack said as air escaped his lips and he settled into the deep chair. "You might have to help me up out of here."

"It wouldn't hurt for you to lose a few pounds, you fat bastard," Nickie said, knowing she could outrun him if she had to. He was basically wedged in the chair.

Hugh Jack adjusted his body for a more comfortable position as he reached into his suit coat and pulled out a pill bottle and a leather case that held three fresh cigars. The case was made of elephant skin and had his initials burned in the center. He extracted one, cut the end, and rolled it between his lips. He placed his drink on the table and with his free hand rolled the cigar as he lit the end, creating an even burn.

He picked up the bottle of pills from the veterinarian, opened it, poured two in his hand, and quickly plopped them in his mouth. He took a long gulp from his old fashioned and smacked his lips.

"I'm waitin'."

Hugh Jack pointed toward the number ten green using his cigar.

"You remember how bad it was raining after I brought you here?"

"Yeah."

"That is the number ten green right there. I found a man's remains that had been buried under the green and was exposed from all the rain. I think I know who they belong to. When the McCowan brothers took my money, they also took a similar suitcase full of those remains with them. I am selling those remains to the person who I think murdered the man who the original remains belong to ... for one hundred thousand dollars. When Paul and Peat stole the original bones, I had to have another set. I happen to know a person who is talented in that area ..."

"You mean a damn grave robber?"

"Yes, a grave robber. I prefer to call him a procurement expert, but in this case, he was a grave robber." Hugh Jack was careful to be completely honest with Nickie.

"I had to replace the bones in order to get the money. That's where the bones came from, I'm not a murderer, I'm not ever going to hurt you." Hugh Jack said as he took the last drink from his Old-Fashioned, draining the very last drop.

"You want another one?" Nickie asked.

"I do, but don't think I can get out of this chair."

"Tell me what to do and I'll make it."

Hugh Jack hollered instructions to Nickie, and she was soon back and handed him the full tumbler.

"So, I could use a little help pulling this little caper off. You interested in making some money?"

"How much?

"Five thousand."

"Holy shit, you serious? Damn, I ain't never seen that kinda money before. What do you need me to do?"

"Well, for starters we're going to need to move up the exchange, so I'll need you to deliver a letter."

Hugh Jack and Nickie sat quietly for several moments as he smoked the rest of his cigar and nursed his drink. Nickie kept stealing short glances toward him, trying to figure out how to ask him a question that had been preying on her mind.

"Can I ask you a question?" Nickie asked quietly, with a serious tone in her voice.

"Sure Darlin'."

"Why ain't you ever made a move on me?"

Hugh Jack stared out onto the golf course, the day ending.

"To be honest, I don't know. I mean normally I would have by now. I've been with women your age before, but there's just something about you. I feel like you've been hurt pretty badly before and I guess I don't want to hurt you further. Hell, I guess I'm growing a conscience ... maybe I am redeemable after all," Hugh Jack said with a quick, uncomfortable laugh.

A slow tear fell down Nickie's cheek and dropped off her chin. She turned her face toward Hugh Jack.

"Besides my daddy, you're the first man that's ever been nice to me. I's kidnapped when I was six, held hostage by a man for a year, and abused every day in ways that people hadn't even made up yet. He took pictures of me naked, made videos, sold me to his friends ... peed on me. My parents died in a car wreck close to a year after I was rescued. I'd been living in foster homes since then, and for ten fuckin' years most of the foster dads and some of the moms took advantage of me. It's just been my whole life, sixteen homes. It's like that's what God put me on this earth for was to be abused and used by people. It's never stopped until now. That's why I've never left here. I feel safe with you."

"Would it be all right if I hugged you?" Hugh Jack asked, his arms held out with tears streaming down his face.

Nickie leaned over her chair and hugged him, but before long, moved to his lap crying, sobbing as if she had never cried before. Pain released from her as if she finally had met a man that didn't want to use her up and throw her away when he was through with her. They stayed like this for several minutes holding each other, not speaking.

Her tears finally drying up. She simply couldn't cry any longer. She sat in Hugh Jack's lap curled up; his arms wrapped around her holding her. They watched the sun slowly begin to disappear behind the pines, the orange globe reflecting from the lake. Bullfrogs started their evening chorus, joined by the katydids. The summer heat burned off the mowed grass as the last of the golfers made their way back to their cart sheds to have one more beer before they had to go home and start a new week. The golf course was still and quiet. They were still and quiet.

"You womanizing piece of shit!"

Hugh Jack's wife stood between the French doors holding a thirty-eight snub-nosed revolver in her hand.

Nickie jumped up and moved to the corner of the deck.

"Who are you?" his wife asked, as if she were meeting the next in a long line of mistresses.

"Nickie."

"You couldn't be over twelve ... she couldn't be over twelve," she said, turning to Hugh Jack. Your other two whores came to the office today looking for money. They found out about each other AND me, and now I come out here and find you with this fresh, young thing."

Hugh Jack tried to get out of the chair. He threw his cigar down, he knocked his drink over, and ice slid across the deck. He could not get his heft out of the chair, he was stuck. Nickie moved to help him.

"You just stay your pretty little self right there," Sheila said, almost sweetly, pointing the gun at Nickie.

"Now Sheila, this isn't wha..."

"You going try to tell me this isn't what it looks like? You here, with a half-clothed pretty, young girl, her bottom hangin' out of those shorts, and you're going try to tell me this isn't what it looks like! You sonofabitch! Daddy tried to tell me about you. Stupid me thought I could change you. I'm done."

With every syllable, Sheila's voice rose louder and louder cracking between the sobbing tears. Every woman she naively forgave him for now made her more and more angry.

"Mam he..."

"Shut up little girl, I guess you're going to tell me that you didn't even know he was married."

"I knew," Nickie said, meekly.

"Oh, so now you been talking about me to all your little whores."

Hugh Jack kept trying to get out of the chair. He was sweating from his effort.

"You don't need to try to get out of that seat. You can just stay right there."

Sheila pulled the thirty-eight up, straightening her arm and pulled the trigger twice, pumping two shells into Hugh Jacks chest and then quietly dropped the gun on the deck, turned, and looked at Nickie.

"You can call the police if you want to, I just don't care anymore," Sheila said, as she quietly walked back through the door and left.

Nickie ran to Hugh Jack, crying.

"No, no, no," Nickie said over and over again. "I'll call the ambulance." Hugh Jack caught her hand and reached in his pocket and gave her two sheets of folded paper.

"Take care of yourself Darlin', keep the money," he said, as he lovingly touched her cheek almost covering half of her face with his massive hand. His hand slowly slid down her cheek as he took his last breath.

Nickie sat quietly sobbing, staring at a man she had come to love, a man who respected her and saw something in her besides a hot, young girl to have sex with, like most of the other men in her life had.

She brought her trembling hand to her lips, kissed it, then placed it on Hugh Jack's mouth.

"You are redeemed."

Nickie stood and started going through Hugh Jack's pockets. She took his keys and found his wallet. She withdrew the cash, wiped his wallet down, and replaced it. She checked his other pants pocket and extracted a roll of cash that would make a horse choke.

She stood and looked at him one more time and said goodbye. She went downstairs into the tack room, removed the hay, stood on the board, pulled the ring, and opened the secret door. She extracted the suitcase, went into the bedroom, and packed the few things she had into her backpack, waited for dark to arrive, and started walking toward the country store.

She arrived at the store and saw Bandit and Huny getting in their van.

"Can you take me to a hotel close by?"

"Sure, hop in," Huny said as she took a gulp of her Miller Lite. "What happened to stayin' at the barn?"

"That just came to an end."

"All good things do, hun."

Bandit stopped the car at the Motorcoach Inn on the outskirts of town. Thirty-two dollars cash, and she had a place for the night—no ID, no credit card, just cash.

Nickie walked down to the convenience store next door and used the pay phone, dialed 911, and made a report.

"They's a dead man on the second-floor deck of the barn by the Beau Chene Country Club. He's been shot. The wife did it, I think her name's Sheila. She was wearin' a long denim skirt and western style shirt, and her hair is up in a bun. She left the gun on the floor after she shot him, you got all that?"

"I do 'mam but …," the operator's voice ended as Nickie hung up the phone.

Night

A long casket lay in the center of the number ten green on a golf course, cloaked in green moss and mildew. A flag waved slowly. The number ten came in and out of sight as it moved back and forth like a snake slowly winding along the ground. Russ stared at it, trying to work out how to putt around it. He walked by it and looked down into the opened casket. Bones wearing a suit made of dollar bills lay in it. It was a simple casket made of pine wood, no interior details, no cushion, no material at all, just plain wood.

Soon the ground around the casket started giving way, disintegrating, gobbling up the casket and the green around it. Russ stood staring at the green and the flag still standing erect, waving as if wind were moving it. He looked down as a pitching wedge appeared in his hand. He used it and chipped the ball over the moat and onto the green near the flag, and it rolled in.

He jumped over the moat from where he stood to retrieve the ball. He hovered in the air, slowly moving toward the flag looking down into the abyss seeing nothing but darkness, floating. Soon a small figure appeared. Clothed flesh, suit made from dollar bills. The figure grew and grew as he drew closer out of the depths of the infinite bottom.

"I wish you were never born," said the hollow voice.

The man, dressed in a suit of money, now stood beside the flag, holding it like a caddy watching a putt nearing its desired place in the bottomless hole.

"Come get your ball," the figure said.

Russ walked to the flag to pick up his ball, looking down into his father's face staring back at him.

Russ woke, drenched in sweat and breathing heavily, sat straight up in the bed. Another morning had come.

CHAPTER TWENTY-TWO

The news hit town early the next morning as Lewiston slowly came to life. Russ spoke to the few shopkeepers who were sweeping in front of their stores as he made his way to the office. He felt them stare at him, as if they knew what he was involved in.

"Have you already heard?" Bubba asked, as he met Russ coming through the front office door.

"Heard what?"

"Hugh Jack is dead."

"What! How?" Russ asked, a look of defeat washing over his face.

"Sheila apparently caught him with a young girl and shot him right then and there."

Russ and Bubba made their way into the office.

"Dammit! Who was the young girl?" Russ asked, aware she might be someone they know.

"Don't know. That's what I've heard Sheila told the police. She's not getting out on bail right now from what I understand."

"Bubba, we've got to get out to the barn at Beau Chene

and his house while Sheila's in jail and find those remains. This is going to be our only chance," Russ pleaded.

"I understand, but we need to let things cool down a couple of days. Cops have been all over the crime scene out there. I'm sure they have the house covered up, too."

"Do me a favor, Bubba. See what else you can find out from your source at the police station. See if they've found an unusual bag of bones that just happened to be laying around," Russ said, as he winked at Bubba.

CHAPTER TWENTY-THREE

Two days passed. Nickie sat in front of the large window in her motel room, numb. She sat in a chair with her knees drawn to her chest, the back of her right hand covering her mouth. She had been unable or more importantly, unwilling to move. Sleep would not come. Exhaustion mediated all of her thoughts. Her head would not clear. It only swirled around one singular thought. She wasn't able to move past the fact that within minutes she had finally found a man, a father, who treated her with respect and love and then he was gone, dead. Just like the others. What took her years to find was gone again. First her father, now Hugh Jack. She was so close.

She asked herself if she was willing to go through this all over again, the time it took her to trust someone ... a decent man who didn't want to use her up and throw her away when they were finished ... the beatings and the drugs when it all got too hard to handle. Her thoughts were far too many. The unanswered questions rattled in her head and would not leave her alone.

She knew Hugh Jack had been a questionable character

in other parts of his life, but she also knew how he treated her, how his last concern was being a redeemed man. Minutes before he took her in his arms and showed her compassion and love, she was scared that he was a murderer. He had a suitcase of someone's bones hidden in a barn, for God's sake.

Had he lived, maybe she could have helped him right some wrongs, fix some things in his life that haunted him; and in turn she could bask in the love and attention she so much craved from a father figure. It had taken her all these years of going through a string of men who used her, to finally find the most unlikely man that could see her pain, that could almost see right through her. He knew she needed something more than a groping, horny old man in her life—a man who had a heart, a sweetness about him.

She wiped her nose and dried the tears. The tears were part selfishness and part compassion.

She stared at the contents of her pockets on her bedside table. The white folded papers lay there. She was too scared to look at it, too scared she would discover tears she thought no longer existed, for a man she just learned to love and trust. She was scared of continuing the longing again, scared of knowing she had something that in an instant was gone.

She stared out of the window before her. A string of people walked up and down the street, drinking occasionally from tall, brown bags that formed the shape of a bottle. The people stopped and talked and shared cigarettes. Some laughed, possibly at a joke. Lone dollar bills and loose change were passed among them as they pooled resources to buy another quart.

Some would share, others wouldn't. The passage of their vices between them kept them complacent until that ended. Then small skirmishes would break out. They pushed and shoved until their egos remained intact and their attention again turned toward the drink and the drugs and the smoke.

The world out her window was one she had been trying to escape her entire life. She didn't want to live in a cheap motel for the rest of her days, relegated to what she was able to do and have by the few dollars in her pocket. She cringed at the thought of what she may have to do to earn those few dollars.

She moved over to the table, angrily grabbed the paper, and returned to her place in front of the window. She carefully opened it and immediately recognized Hugh Jack's handwriting. She brushed her hand over the paper as if she were touching him. Her eyes clouded with tears again, and she dotted them with a tissue, careful to dot around the raw, swollen parts.

There were two pieces of paper. The first detailed the plan for the exchange of money and bones. The second was basically a list of locations showing where he had money stashed and how much. The majority was out at his house.

The expression on her face turned from anger to shock as she read the list. Twenty thousand, fake pipe in the store room in the garage. Fifteen thousand in the fake air conditioner return vent in bedroom of the pool house. Thirty thousand false end on the bookcase. There was fifty thousand in the barn under the plank in the third stall on the left. She glanced over the word gold as she quickly made her way down the list. The list went on and on with different amounts scattered here and there. On the back there was also a plan for the exchange between Russ and Hugh Jack at the warehouse. One hundred thousand dollars would be exchanged for the remains. As she reached just over the midway point, it had grown to over half a million. It was all hers; she just had to go get it.

No wonder Hugh Jack didn't act so concerned about losing the money to the McCowan brothers. That was just a drop in the bucket. He sure was stubborn about giving it up though. Greed... that was just greed.

CHAPTER TWENTY-FOUR

Russ and Bubba sat in their office waiting for two more hours until nightfall. Prepared to search the barn near the country club as well as Hugh Jack's home and any out buildings on his property. They went over the checklist. They confirmed Sheila was still in jail and would be for a while.

There was no other family living with them, they confirmed that. No dogs inside the house. All of Hugh Jack's horses and dogs were at the barn at Beau Chene. The house and property there should be free and clear. They each packed flashlights, small crowbars, and ski masks.

As Bubba mixed them both a drink, they heard the mail slot in the door creak slowly open and then fall shut. They looked at each other and made their way quickly to the door, noticing a 3 X 5 index card on the floor in front of them. Russ bent down to pick it up.

IT'S STILL ON, SAME LOCATION, TONIGHT.

"Who the hell is this?" Russ yelled, throwing the card

back to the floor. "Who the hell knows about this besides Hugh Jack?"

Russ flung open the door and looked up and down the street. Main Street was empty.

"Sheila's in jail," Bubba said, trying to narrow the list. "Hugh Jack doesn't have kids. He really doesn't have any relatives that I know of. All his old runners he used in the law firm moved on a long time ago."

"It's not like him to have a partner to split the money with, unless…"

"Unless what?" Bubba asked, his eyes wide as if he were thinking the same thing Russ was about to say.

"Unless the cops found the bones, know about the exchange and are confirming what they think they know. This could be a set-up," Russ said, suddenly concerned.

"So, are you saying we don't show up?" Bubba asked, unsettled at the uncertainty of the unknown.

"No, I say we stick with our plan. But as a means of precaution, I think you should get there earlier and be in the garage waiting. If the police are involved, they will be doing the same thing. One cop wouldn't be coming to the exchange by himself. He would have back up. You see anybody, slip out the side door and alert me. We'll call it off. If I don't see you before the timed meeting, I'll go ahead with it," Russ said as he rubbed his hands together nervously, uncertain of his plan but bound by time.

Nickie sat at her small table in her motel room making a list. A roach crawled across the paper she took notes on. She was nervous about the impending meeting; her stomach turning flips.

Concentration was hard with the murmured shouting from a light skirmish in the parking lot in front of her. She counted the money she had left over, three thousand dollars until she could get her hands on the rest.

A small used car lot was located directly across the street from her motel. She would need a car. Either of Hugh Jack's would be too risky and would draw too much attention.

She walked across the street past the drunks and into the office of "Two Brothers Used Cars." Sam Perkins was on the phone ordering takeout. Nickie stood in front of him with her arms crossed, looking impatient. He finally hung up the phone and stood, extending his hand toward Nickie.

"Sam Perkins, how you doin'?"

Nickie kept her arms crossed.

"My name's Nickie. I got fifteen hundred for a reliable car. What you got?"

"Not much for fifteen hundred. Let's go take a look."

Sam and Nickie stepped out of the office and stood in front of a long row of cars and trucks, all clean but obviously used.

"So, which one's in my price range?" Nickie asked as she set her eye on a red 240ZX.

She walked over to the 240 and looked inside. The seats were torn and the dash was cracked.

"That one just came in. I haven't had a chance to get it detailed yet; plus, it'll run you around four thousand."

Sam took Nickie to the end of the line of cars and pointed toward a small black Ford truck with a camper shell covering the bed.

"This one is eighteen hundred, about eighty thousand miles, runs good."

Nickie sat in the truck; it was clean. She had never had her own vehicle before, and this one seemed to fit her small frame well. She cranked it and turned on the radio and found a clear signal on an FM station. "Smells Like Teen Spirit," roared as she found the signal.

"I'll give you sixteen hundred," Nickie said, smiling at Sam, flirting trying to save herself two hundred dollars.

"Sixteen fifty and we have a deal," Sam said as he stuck out his hand.

"I ain't gonna have no gas money if I give you sixteen fifty. Please take sixteen."

"Okay. Let's do it. Come on, and I'll get your paperwork started."

Nickie stood in the doorway of Two Brothers Used Cars waiting for her paperwork. She watched across the street in front of her room as a police car pulled up and two officers got out. They knocked on the door and peered inside the window. They stood outside looking around the parking lot. They made their way back to the motel office and stayed in there for less than a minute. From there they went inside the laundromat. They reappeared and got back into their cruiser and left.

"I need to hurry."

"I just need your signature right here and here," Sam said pointing to the places in the paperwork that made the truck Nickie's.

He counted the one-hundred-dollar bills and handed Nickie the keys.

"It's all yours."

"Thank you."

Nickie got in the truck, cranked it, and drove across the street. She quickly went in her room, grabbed the suitcase and her bag, loaded her truck, and drove down the street. She felt free. Free to roam anywhere. Suddenly her possibilities were endless.

CHAPTER TWENTY-FIVE

Russ dropped Bubba off two blocks from the warehouse. He walked the two blocks and found the same side door he and Russ had gone through a few days earlier. He carefully stepped inside, making sure the room was empty. He quickly made his way around the building, getting the lay of the land, making sure no one else had the same idea as he and Russ.

Satisfied all was clear, he took his position in a dark corner to the right of the side door and waited.

"I'm here and settled," Bubba said as he lifted the walkie talkie close to his mouth.

"Good, I'll let you know when I see someone approaching," Russ whispered, careful to hold the button down on the side.

As Bubba sat and waited in the hot, dark corner of the metal building, he began sweating and suddenly needed to use the bathroom.

"I need to use the bathroom," Bubba whispered into the walkie talkie.

"Just pee in the corner, we can't take a chance on anyone seeing you."

The hushed conversation hung in the air as if it were stuck in the heat of the day.

Bubba walked to the corner and started to empty his bladder. The steady stream hit the tin wall, reverberating and echoing so loud it sounded like a woodpecker trying hard to bore a hole in the galvanized tin.

Midstream, Russ's voice cracked into the walkie talkie and startled Bubba. He jerked, and his walkie talkie slid from under his armpit onto the floor and slid across the concrete. He was just finishing and zipping up when the door began to open. He grabbed the walkie talkie and slid back to his dark corner that now smelled of urine.

"Shhh, they're here," Bubba whispered responding to Russ.

The door opened, and a black Ford Ranger drove into the dark garage.

Bubba watched in disbelief as a young, petite, blonde girl got out of the driver's side and walked to the door, grabbed a rope, and pulled the door down.

Who in the hell is that?

The girl stood at the rear of the Ford Ranger and lifted the camper door, pulling out a large leather suitcase. She pulled a piece of paper from her front pocket and started reading. She looked around the building and up toward the top of the stair case, folded the paper, and returned it to her front pocket. She looked around the dark room for a second time and shut the camper. She started walking backwards up the stairs to the loft, handling the suitcase, sliding it on each step of the stairs. She finally made it to the top after stopping to rest a couple of times. Finally, she dragged it through the door and into the room that housed the pulley system. Bubba heard her plop the suitcase on top of the metal platform.

Russ's walkie talkie squawked, "You ain't gon' believe this. A black Ford Ranger just pulled in with a young petite blonde girl driving. She's got the suitcase upstairs. She's alone," Bubba said, almost laughing.

"One of Hugh Jack's harem I suppose. You grab her when she comes back down with the money, and I'll meet y'all in there," Russ said, relieved it wasn't the police.

"Ten-four," Bubba said, as he made his way to the truck and hid himself against the passenger's rear tire.

After placing the bag on top of the platform, she pulled the paper from her front pocket. It contained a to-do list that was part of Hugh Jack's careful planning.

After placing the bag on the platform, lock the handle of the suitcase to the wire on the platform. This will give me time to get back down to my truck and get away while he is still trying to get the lock off.

She shoved the paper back into her pocket and closed the lock on the top handle of the suitcase. She locked it exactly as Hugh Jack instructed, and then she waited.

The front door slowly opened. She could see a small line of light as she peered through the crack in the pulley system. The line darkened again as she heard the door close.

"I'm here," Russ said looking up into the ceiling.

Nickie froze. She didn't know she would have to talk. This guy was just supposed to put the money on the platform and not talk. There was nothing in the plan about talking. If she opened her mouth, it could blow the whole deal, so she just kept quiet. She looked through the crack, trying to catch a glimpse of the person below. Soon the platform with the suitcase on it began to descend. She backed up so she wouldn't be seen as the money began to ascend toward her. She was careful to stay in the dark, waiting patiently on more money than she had ever seen before.

The platform quickly clicked in place, and she grabbed the duffle bag. It was heavy as well. Her planned fast escape was slowed as she hadn't considered how much one hundred thousand dollars weighed. The twenty pounds of flour that Russ had added to the bottom of the bag was proving hard to manage.

Bubba now stood with his back against the wall of the stair case. It took an excruciatingly long time for her to pull the bag down the stairs, but she finally made it to the bottom. She stood doubled over resting her hands on her knees when she heard the crack of a walkie talkie.

"She locked the damn suitcase to the platform. Get her!"

Nickie looked up. Bubba stood in front of her. She kicked him in the groin and started running but didn't get far. Bubba picked her up, kicking, screaming, and flailing. She bit his arm and elbowed him in the side of the head. He dropped her and fell to his knees. She reached the door and pulled it opened and ran into Russ. Russ dropped the suitcase and grabbed her in a bear hug.

"Don't let her get near your nuts," Bubba said in a weakened voice.

"Calm down, we just want to talk. We're not going to hurt you," Russ said still dodging the attempted blows. "We aren't going to hurt you."

"Let me go, you dumbass redneck!"

"If you keep screaming, you're going to attract people here that none of us want. Shut up!" Russ said more forcefully.

"Put me down!"

"Okay, I'm going to put you down. Just relax. We just want to talk, okay." Russ said as he loosened his grip.

As soon as Nickie was free, she turned around to Russ and slapped him.

"Don't ever touch me like that again, you freak."

Russ stood in front of Nickie, his eyes watering from the slap, his cheek stinging, and his hands held up in surrender.

"I need to get the hell out of here," Nickie said, slowly backing away from the two of them.

"Look, we heard what happened to Hugh Jack. We just want to know how you came across what's in this suitcase. What do you know about it?" Russ asked calmly.

"I know there's some damn bones in there, and as bad as you want the damn things back, I'm thinking you or this silverback gorilla here killed whoever is in that suitcase. And I guess now that you know that I know, I'm dead, too."

"We're not going to kill you. It's not what you think. Look at me. I'm thirty-one years old. Do you know how long it takes for a body to become dirt, nothing to be left but bone?" Russ asked.

He pulled out his wallet and showed her his driver's license.

"See I would have had to be sixteen when this guy died, I'm not some kind of serial killer. I don't want to hurt you."

"What about the money?" Nickie asked. "I really need some money to get out of this place and move on down the road."

Bubba walked over to the duffle bag full of "money" and opened it. Four, five-pound sacks of flour lay in the bottom of the bag.

"We know or rather knew Hugh Jack; we knew he had what's in the suitcase. We were never going to pay one hundred thousand dollars to him. I just needed to get these back," Russ said, waiting for the avalanche of screaming and cussing to begin.

"Why do you want these back so bad? If you were fifteen when this person was killed and all this time has passed, why do you want these so bad? What's the story? If I ain't gettin' no money, you at least owe me that," Nickie demanded.

Russ looked at Bubba and stared at him. He threw his head back and walked off with his hands on his hips exhausted at the prospect of having to relive his past life again, relive his recent dreams.

"It just never will end," Russ said.

"What ain't gon' end?" Nickie asked, now intrigued with Russ's story.

Russ walked back over to Bubba. "Should I tell her?"

"Well, somebody better tell me something, or I'm going to the damn police."

"Don't do it," Bubba said to Russ. "Just don't."

Russ stood in front of Bubba. They stared into each other's eyes. Bubba slightly shook his head.

"Don't do it, son."

Russ turned and looked at Nickie, her eyes darting back and forth from Russ to Bubba.

Russ walked over to the suitcase and stood in front of it, rubbing his chin with his index finger, thinking. He bent down, his hand hovered above the zipper. His fingers flexed as if he was unsure. He stood and walked away from the case.

"What in the hell are you doing? Damn, shit or get off the pot. What are we doing here?" Nickie asked, tired of the unknown, tired of standing in the hot garage.

Russ moved back to the suitcase, unzipped it, and flung

open the lid, moving backwards at the same time. His eyes filled with tears from the emotion of it all, from the memories, from the anger, from the dreams that just wouldn't end.

"That son of a bitch has never been buried, he won't stay gone … you bastard!"

Russ was crying and pacing the floor. His face contorted into a mask of resentment and fear. His fingers ran through his hair—squeezing, pulling.

"It won't end, Bubba," Russ said, as he buried his head in Bubba's chest, sobbing.

As Bubba comforted Russ, he looked at Nickie, his own eyes filling with tears. Memories of the past came flooding back. Cappy, all the boys, Effie and Jaimey, all those great years. Now he stood with Russ, who was like a son to him, hurting constantly, and he couldn't fix it.

Nickie's eyes were wide. It was always uncomfortable to see grown men cry. It also made her realize she wasn't standing in front of two murderers, just two men who loved each other and obviously had a story to tell.

Bubba stared down at the remains in the suitcase. He pulled Russ away from him and walked closer.

"Something's not right."

"What do you mean?" Russ asked, wiping his face.

"Randy was tall, over six feet, right?"

"Yeah, so?" Russ asked trying to follow Bubba's thought process.

"Who's Randy?" Nickie asked.

"Look at that femur. That's not the femur of a man who stood over six feet tall," Bubba said as he looked up at Russ. "This ain't Randy."

"Who is Randy?" Nickie asked again, frustrated she was being ignored.

Russ stood and turned to Nickie. "Randy was my father. He was an abusive drunk who beat me and my mother. He spit on my mom. He never worked. My mom became a prostitute to support all of us because that sorry piece of shit drank all the time and gambled all of our money away."

Nickie stared at Russ Shocked. The room became silent, no one spoke a word.

"I killed him to protect my mom and me, and I buried him..." Russ was interrupted by Nickie.

"Under the number ten green. And when the rains came, it washed the green away exposing your dad's remains. Hugh Jack told me how he found the skeleton," Nickie said, finishing Russ's story.

"So, you knew?" Russ asked, confused.

"I know what I just told you. He didn't tell me who you were. I know something else. I know where your bones are," Nickie said.

Bubba and Russ looked at each other.

"I'll tell you, but you got to get me out of this shed. It's too damn hot in here," Nickie said.

Russ grabbed a rag lying on the ground and wiped the suitcase down.

"Leave that. I don't want those things near me ... Bubba, will you drive her truck and meet us at Mom's? The office will be too busy to take her there. She'll ride with me," Russ said.

"Hell, Russ," Bubba said. "I can't fit in that damn little bitty truck."

"Okay, you take mine. She and I will ride in hers. See you at Mom's.

"That's better," Bubba said as he picked up their bag of "money" and walked to the truck.

CHAPTER TWENTY-SIX

Turtle McCowan paid the balance in cash for the new white Corvette, after trading in the black one. He wanted the red one, but red drew too much attention from the Cops. With the trade-in, the new Corvette cost him thirty thousand dollars. He parted with more of the cash at a men's clothing store and grabbed one of the fat rolls to stick in his pocket for the bar tonight.

Two days earlier he checked into the most expensive hotel he had ever stayed in, a Hampton Inn. The suitcase and the duffle bags were stacked inside the closet, crammed into the tight space, hidden as well as they could be.

With the new clothes and the new car and a roll of cash that would choke a horse, he was ready to find a new woman. Turtle only knew of the seedy bars and the type of women who inhabited such places. That is where he was most comfortable, the soft white underbelly of life.

These bars held women he thought had no hope and craved attention from any man who would look their way. This was the last stop for women who had started at the top and worked their way down until finding acceptance, attention, and love all from the wrong type of men. These women weren't able to attract the men who sat at The Peabody Hotel bar in Memphis. Instead, they attracted men at bars attached to the side of cheap motels. The bars that were the seediest, the ones in the wrong part of town, lit mainly by neon.

It was there that Turtle felt most comfortable as well. Tonight, that type of bar was where Turtle would stand out —in a room full of men who could barely afford a couple of drinks. It was where he could flash his money, buy the house a round, and hopefully leave with a woman on his arm, one who would sit beside him and be impressed by his new Corvette.

It was dusk when Turtle pulled up to the "South Shall Rise Again" bar and social club. The bar was housed in a large defunct cotton gin. The white paint had been flaking and peeling for years, turning the structure into a dark wooden building and making for a more ominous look. It stood singular in the middle of a field toward the end of a long river road that provided plenty of parking. Few lights shone on the outside, just two on either side of the entrance. Shining down on two grown men full of muscle and vacant of patience, checking ages and skin color.

The parking lot was beginning to fill, mostly pickups and company work trucks. He parked the Corvette on the end of the row away from the others, trying to avoid scratches, dings, and possibly keys from the jealous types. He walked by a group of college-aged boys having a pissing contest, weaving from a day of drinking that started at noon.

As he approached the door, he showed his I.D., and the gorilla on the left patted him down.

"No knives, guns or weapons of any kind?" the Gorilla asked, as he thrust his hand up each thigh.

He walked through the door and was met by a much smaller man wearing a Bocephus t-shirt and a straw cowboy hat.

"Stick out your arm," he said around a plastic straw protruding from his mouth, the exposed end mutilated by nervous energy.

He stamped Turtle's arm. The initials SSRA glowed in the dark.

Healthy girls walked around with trays floating above their heads. They were periodically doused with a spritz of water from the bartender, making transparent an already thin t-shirt. It was as close to being a topless bar as the law would allow. Four times a night the girls would stand on the bar and line up in front of the cage while some lucky drunk purchased the right to spray them down by buying a round of drinks for the bar's employees.

The man in the cage was closing in on seventy-nine. Rex sat on a stool and sang dirty ditties mainly about women in various stages of undress and illicit activity.

As they danced in front of him, he brought the crowd to a fever pitch singing, "Bounce, bounce, bounce ..."

Four times a night, every night, the bar patrons sang in unison, led by Rex, the "bouncing titty song" while the girls who were getting sprayed did their best impression of real strippers.

Turtle made his way to the bar. As he did, he looked to his left noticing a line of ten pool tables surrounded by men who had come to The South Shall Rise Again straight from work. They still wore the dirt from the ground they dug, and the grease from the cars they serviced.

They played pool beside fraternity brothers dressed in

clean jeans and khakis, wearing their letters on sweaters and caps and wherever else they could advertise. Cute coeds hung off them and held their pool cues when they disappeared to take a leak.

And then Turtle spotted what he came for—the women lined up almost like cattle at a sale, hanging off their bar stools trying their best to look sexy, needy, and ready. Their hair was fixed, their tans brown. White halter tops and short shorts advertised their willingness to be plowed with drinks, taken home and used, and thrown out the next morning.

Desperation claimed their faces. Their approach to men was like watching a movie with bad actors. So uncertain of themselves, their self-confidence shot long ago, they needed and wanted love and attention, and Turtle McCowan was in the house.

He moved toward the women and stood in the center of them. He stood close to the bar and watched with his peripheral vison to see if any eyes were on him. He pulled out the roll and popped the rubber band a couple of times to gain their attention. He slipped off the rubber band and peeled a one-hundred-dollar bill from the top, exposing another one-hundred-dollar bill below it.

"Would you like a beer?" Turtle asked as he turned to the brunette sitting beside him, nonchalantly holding the bill between his index and middle fingers.

"Sure."

"Bud, okay?"

"I'd rather have a Miller Lite. Girls got to watch her figure, unless you want to do the watchin', in which case I'll have a Bud."

Turtle ordered two Budweiser's and turned all of his

attention to the brunette. He leaned on the bar on his elbow, still popping the rubber band on the wad of cash.

"What's your name?"

"Gloria, but my last boyfriend just called me Glo and most of my close friends do."

"What about you? What's your name?"

"My momma calls me Paul, but my friends call me Turtle."

"Turtle. Why Turtle?"

"It's a long story; want to get out of here?"

"Let's go."

Turtle and Glo walked arm in arm through the crowd. Rex was behind the chicken wire singing a song about particular parts of a woman's body. Women poked their bras and panties through the holes in the wire. Half empty beer bottles were thrown toward Rex, bouncing off the loose chicken wire, spraying those close by. Men and their dates danced as close as their bodies would allow.

A group of college-aged boys were nursing egos and puffing bravado, mouthing at each other, the beginning of a fight that was quickly spilling outside.

Turtle and Glo slipped by the boys and through the front door past the gorillas. After walking half way to his car they stopped and kissed. Turtle had Glo backed up against a truck as they slid along its side toward the tail-gate. He popped the tailgate down and lifted her onto the bed when a beer bottle caught Turtle on the side of his face.

He stood dazed; blood poured from above his left eye. He felt the blood with his hand, still unsure of what just happened. A fist followed the beer bottle, finding his jaw. His head popped back, and he fell backwards, unable to break his fall.

A hand found its way into his front pants pocket and

extracted the roll of cash. After the rest of his pockets were gone through and his new watch was taken from his wrist, the figure stood and popped the rubber band after he strapped his new watch to his wrist.

"Never flaunt your money, son," the man said.

He turned to Gloria and asked her if she wanted a beer. Like nothing at all had happened, she jumped down from the truck, zipped her pants up, and held the man's hand at the promise of a free drink.

CHAPTER TWENTY-SEVEN

Bubba arrived first at Jaimey's house. He walked through the front door and helped himself to a beer from her refrigerator. He was followed by Russ and Nickie.

"Mom," Russ shouted toward the upstairs.

"Coming."

"Would you like something to drink?" Russ asked Nickie, as he watched Bubba down his beer.

"A beer would be good right now."

"My nerves are shot. Give me another one," Bubba said to Russ as he put his hands up to catch another beer.

"You got a bathroom I could use really quick?" Nickie asked, looking around the house.

Russ showed her to the bathroom and turned the light on for her. Jaimey made it down the stairs and into the kitchen. She looked at Bubba who was still covered in sweat, looking haggard and tired. Russ had his head down on the table exhausted.

"You don't look like things went according to plan," Jaimey said, her hand over her mouth.

Russ saw Nickie enter the room.

"Mom, this is Nickie; Nickie this is ..."

"Jaimey ... a mommy," Nickie said as her knees buckled and her body went limp and she fainted."

Russ and Jaimey rushed over to her.

"How does she know my name?" asked Jaimey, as she frantically moved to Nickie's head and laid it on her lap. "Get me a cold rag, quick. Who is she? How does she know who I am?"

"I don't know. She has been living with Hugh Jack, and she knows about the bones. It's a long story. She showed up at the exchange today," Russ said excitedly, unable to think straight.

Jaimey wiped Nickie's forehead and face, gently rubbing the cold rag on her skin.

"She such a little thing," Jaimey said as she twirled the rag in the air cooling it some more.

"Nickie ... Nickie baby, wake up. Wake up, Sweetie," Jaimey said, as she looked up at Russ and Bubba. "Y'all back up a little bit. You're hovering around her like she's an alien or something."

Jaimey started to say her name again. While gently shaking her, she woke, looked into Jaimey's eyes and immediately hugged her. She was squeezing Jaimey's neck tight, and Jaimey didn't know what to do but hug her back. Jaimey looked up at Bubba and Russ, perplexed and confused. Nickie finally let go and sat up.

"Do you remember me? Do you know who I am? Look at me real hard," Nickie said, as she turned, still sitting, facing Jaimey. She pulled her hair back from her face as if that would help. "It's Madison. Madison Nicole Vowell."

Jaimey's mouth dropped open, her eyes filled with tears; she covered her mouth. She sat sobbing, planting her face into the floor. All of her strength leaving her body. She sat back up and touched Nickie's face, and Nickie held her hand there.

Jaimey stood the both of them up, and she held her tight, hugging her. They stayed that way locked in an embrace for several silent minutes.

Russ began crying, now understanding that before him was the same Madison that Jaimey had rescued from her abductor. She was the same little girl they oddly dropped off down the street from her house. The same little girl he watched knock on the front door of her own house then watching her mother collapse when she saw her. Who gathered her up in her arms seeming to never let go. The little girl she saved from more tortured abuse, and probably saved her life. The same little girl who pointed at their car just before Jaimey sped away.

Jaimey had told Russ the story a million times. Now here she was, a small, crumbled body broken from a hard life, reunited with the woman who gave her young life back to her.

"Do you go by Nickie now or do I call you Madison?" Jaimey asked, brushing a stray strand of hair from Nickie's face. "How did you get here, how did you come back to me?"

"Hugh Jack picked me up on the highway down on the coast. I've been living at his barn."

"He didn't try to …," Jaimey probed, making sure Hugh Jack had not tried to hurt or abuse her in any way.

"No, he didn't. He actually was a very decent man, the first man, since my daddy, who treated me like his little girl. He was sweet and kind. He never tried laying a hand on me." Nickie buried her head in Jaimey's chest and softly sobbed. "I think he wanted to make a change in his life.

Before he died, he talked about being redeemed. He was sweet to me. He said he could see that I had been hurt in the past, and that's why he never tried to do anything with me. He saw something in me that I didn't know I showed people. Maybe something only you would understand."

Jaimey placed Nickie's head back into her chest and hugged her. Her mind returned to the day and time when she first saw Nickie—dirty, still dressed in her school uniform, appearing to her in that dark, nasty hellhole, staring at the ground. She had been used up at the tender age of seven. She had seen and felt things most people never see or feel.

"I saw the pictures, well, just a few of them," Nickie said, her eyes moving up toward Jaimey's face as if she would understand.

"Pictures?"

"He took pictures of me with other men that he sold or rather rented me to. Years later when I was in my fourth foster home, the police arrested this man, who had a ton of kiddie porn, and I was in some of them."

"Wait, you were in foster homes. What about your parents, your gorgeous mom, your beautiful home?"

She exhaled, and her childhood flooded from her mouth like poison being poured by a disgruntled wife. It came out fast and hard like it was her plan for it to be the last time to be told, unpleasant all the while.

She told Jaimey about her parents' car wreck and their death and her only living grandmother who died only three months after her parents. No siblings, no aunts, no uncles, nobody. She became a ward of the state, in and out of foster homes her entire life from that point on and abused in most of them.

Nickie and Jaimey could not let each other go; they held each other, now exhausted, resting on the couch.

"I hate to interrupt, but you said you had information about the bones and about Hugh Jack," Russ said, torn between needing to resolve this tension hanging over his head and the scene that just unfolded before him.

"Can we talk in the morning?" Nickie asked, groggily, falling asleep as Jaimey motioned for the conversation to wait.

CHAPTER TWENTY-EIGHT

"Hey get up before I run over your ass."

Turtle felt a boot rocking back and forth on his chest. He had been out cold for hours. Blood had dried on the side of his head where the beer bottle shattered in a thousand pieces.

"I need you to move away from my truck. Get up you drunk bastard," a form standing above Turtle said.

Turtle slowly rolled to his side to start standing when two arms found their way under his, pulling him up. His head started spinning when they did. It was too fast, and he vomited and fell again. Turtle felt hands in each arm pit again and then familiar voices.

"Damn, Turtle, who the hell beat your ass?"

Turtle looked up at two dark figures standing against an even darker sky. The pain wouldn't allow his one good eye to focus, and the other had drops of blood still flowing over it.

"Turtle, you okay?"

"Bandit, is that you ... Huny, is that y'all?" Turtle asked, confused. "Y'all are the last two people I expected to see here. What the hell are y'all doin here?"

"One of them college kids from Lewiston that goes to Ole Miss told us about this place. Said we could sell some weed up here. I've been doin all the work tonight. Huny's been a throwin' up all night, cain't hold no beer."

"I can, too," Huny protested.

"Ain't done it. I been pickin' you up all night," said Bandit.

Turtle sat, holding his head before trying to stand again.

"This pain is the worst I've ever felt."

Turtle sat on a small knoll, elbows propped on his knees, holding his head in his hands. He lightly touched the cut, blood still flowing. He knew he needed stiches. He thrust his hand in his right pocket and felt for his keys. Nothing. He checked his left side. Nothing there as well. He suddenly remembered he put them in his back pocket. Leaning on one side, he finally felt his keys and took them out of his pocket.

Huny, Bandit, and Turtle sat together and watched the last of the employees leave, the lights finally turned out. The gorillas no longer stood by the front door. Turtle decided to stand. He was still dizzy and unsteady on his feet.

"How about y'all walk me to my car?"

They each stood on either side of Turtle and took an arm.

"Come on young'un," Bandit said, as he stuck his half-burned cigarette between his lips.

As they walked toward his car, they all stumbled from exhaustion and drunken dizziness. Huny fell twice; she was no help to Bandit as he tried to get them both to the car.

They finally reached Turtle's Corvette and leaned him against it. Bandit rested his hand in the center of Turtle's chest to hold him up.

"Ewwwee! That's a pretty thang right there!" Bandit said as he stuck the key in the door. "Where's Peat? I don't never see one of y'all without the other."

Turtle was tired of hearing Bandit talk and was thankful Huny didn't feel well, because she talked more than he did. With every syllable Bandit spoke, Turtle felt worse and increasingly irritated. He wasn't expecting so many questions about Peat. He would never tell what happened. He knew he would have to live with the questions and the guilt.

The night didn't go as planned. He had hoped he would have been back in Southaven at the Hampton Inn and in bed with the brunette a long time ago. Turtle began wondering if she had been in on the attack the whole time.

Bandit eased him into his car. Turtle was concerned about bleeding on his white leather interior.

Instead of going to the emergency room, he decided to go to the hotel first and see just how bad the cut was. He placed his hand flatly against his jaw hoping the slight pressure would reduce the pain. He needed ice, bandages, and pain reliever.

"Where are you two staying tonight?"

"We were going to head on back home, why?" Bandit asked, eager to hear what Turtle had to offer.

He reached in the glove compartment where he stashed a few hundred-dollar bills, "just in case," and handed two to Bandit.

"How about y'all let me buy y'all a room tonight and you two go get me some bandages and medicine and stuff to fix my head with?"

Bandit looked at Huny, her eyes were closing for the night. "Sounds good. Where you stayin'?"

"The Hampton Inn on Fifty-five. Room 113."

"We'll see you in a few, young'un."

Night

The small white dot appeared in the blackness again just as it had so many times before, growing larger and larger as if it were getting closer. The one light grew into two, still surrounded by darkness, slowly inching nearer and nearer. The yellow lines in the center of the highway shone bright, framed by the two white round headlamps.

A white figure lacking flesh sat in the driver's seat, its bones moving as if driving. The right boney hand raised a beer to his mouth. Beer spilled out of the mouth and throughout the bones, flooding the seat.

In the bed of the truck were suitcases stacked higher than the truck, flying open as the truck picked up speed and made its way down the road. As each suitcase flew open, a skeleton jumped out and onto the road, running, one after the other until all the suitcases were gone, no longer filling the bed of the truck.

The driver pulled up, floating in the golden liquid. The bottomless beer continued flooding the truck cab. As the door opened, the beer flowed from the truck. The skeleton hopped out, his hands hovering around his hip bones as if keeping a pair of pants from falling down. The skeleton walked toward him.

"I'm lost. You can't find me. You can't find me. You better start looking. Don't give up. Keep looking. You're going to be in trouble. You're going to be caught."

Russ's eyes opened. His chest was heaving, his breathing heavy. He turned and looked out the window. The sky was orange, slowly introducing white light into the day. One more night had come and gone.

CHAPTER TWENTY-NINE

ubba had his crew at Beau Chene at daylight. The footing for the retaining wall had been dug, formed, and poured the day before. He walked onto the new construction and stared down into the woods beyond the green. The rebar now stood straight and tall. Bubba considered the progress they had made in such a short period of time. He asked himself why he didn't insist on building a retaining wall when he and Russ did the original work. He knew the main reason was money. There just wasn't enough to pay for it back then. If he had only insisted, they wouldn't be in this current predicament. He did think about the dirt work holding, but a buried body under the green was the furthest thing from his mind.

Bubba was lost in thought, thinking about all the events that had transpired in the last couple of days. It was hard for him to believe that what took place sixteen years earlier was affecting them all now. The dead truly continue to live.

Bubba's brain finally heard his name called from down near the retaining wall foundation.

"Mr. Bubba, look!"

Bubba glanced down at Jose', one of his foremen. He made his way to the top of the green with his hand held out flat.

"What's that?" Bubba asked as he stood waiting for him to deliver an arrowhead or fossil.

"It is someone's gold tooth," Jose' said, as he poured the tooth into Bubba's hand.

Bubba jerked away, sending the tooth to the ground. Jose' bent down to pick it up, laughing, and tried handing the tooth to Bubba again.

"Just put it on the golf cart," Bubba said, trying to regain his composure.

Jose' did and went back to work. Bubba stared at the gold cap knowing it could only be Randy's. He grabbed a plastic sack that once held ice and with his pen scraped the tooth into the plastic bag and wrapped it tightly. He considered what he should do with it. Should he even tell Russ?

CHAPTER THIRTY

Russ sat at Jaimy's breakfast table nursing a cup of coffee, unable to eat. Nervous energy coursed through his body.

"When will Jim be back from his conference?" Russ asked Jaimey. "You know Bubba is great, and I'm thankful for his help with all of this, but sometimes I feel like I need to talk to Jim. I feel like we're keeping him in the dark about all of this. How late did y'all stay up last night? I'm going to have to go wake her. I can't stand this any longer."

Russ stood and began walking toward the stairs when he heard a door creak upstairs and saw Nickie start down. She had one of his old golf shirts on and a pair of panties.

"Nickie, sweetie, go put some shorts on, okay? Then come on down and I'll have breakfast ready for you," Jaimey said, as her mind retreated to her days spent as a call girl. She remembered how prancing around half dressed didn't bother her either. It meant attention, just the wrong kind.

"Jim will be back soon. You need to relax. Bubba and I are here, and we will see this through with you," Jaimey said, reassuring Russ.

Within minutes, Nickie was sitting at the breakfast table. She placed two pieces of bacon on top of a pancake and drowned them in syrup. She rolled the pancake around the bacon and placed the end of it in her mouth, syrup dripping from her lips.

"Okay, I can't wait any longer, please tell me," Russ said, finished with his forced patience. "Where are they?"

Nickie moved her mouth down closer to her plate trying hard to keep the syrup from Russ's shirt.

"Turtle."

"Turtle?"

"Turtle and Peat ... brothers," Nickie said, mumbling with a full mouth.

"McCowan, the McCowan brothers?"

"I guess," Nickie said, after taking another large bite.

She was eating as if she hadn't eaten in days.

"Did one of them have a scar on his chest and neck, like a burn scar?"

"Peat had a scar. Don't know how he got it though. Ain't never seen nobody get burned before."

"So, what you're telling me is, Turtle and Peat McCowan have the remains?"

"They got them, when they got the money."

"What money?" Russ asked, remaining confused.

"They come in Hugh Jack's barn with guns, screaming about money that Hugh Jack cheated their daddy out of from some old legal case."

"Sounds like Hugh Jack," Jaimey said as she moved her chair closer to Nickie.

"They took us out to this place out in the woods, real nasty, turtle shells all over the place, crappy old house; they made us get naked and walked us out to this clearin'. They sprayed me down with skeeter dope and strung Hugh Jack between two trees by his hands. They said he was getting chigger bites and stuck poison ivy all up his ass and rubbed it all over his chest and in his arm pits. He laid in the bed naked for days after that, scratchin' hisself bloody."

"So how did they find out about the money," Jaimey asked.

"Well Hugh Jack took the pain and itchin' as long as he could, but when Peat started to rape me, he stopped him and told Turtle he would take them to the money. He had the suitcase with the bones in it hid in the same place as the money. They got it all."

"So, the McCowan brothers have the bones," Russ said, throwing his napkin on the table as he got up.

"Who has them?" Bubba asked as he walked into the kitchen.

"Turtle...ah, Paul and Peat McCowan," Russ said, repeating himself.

"Well, that'll be easy getting them back. Hey, I need to see you," Bubba said, as he motioned Russ to leave the kitchen.

"What's up?"

"I have struggled with telling you this, but thought it would be better to tell you than not," Bubba said as he pulled the plastic bag from his back pocket, handing it to Russ.

"What's this?"

"We found it at number ten green. It's a gold tooth," Bubba said, as he dropped the tooth into Russ's flat hand.

Russ jerked his hand back, dropping the wad of plastic. Bubba picked it up.

"I did the same thing. What do you want me to do with it?"

"Don't tell Mom; just throw it away. Surprised the

bastard didn't pull it to sell for beer money. Just throw it away, but not in this house."

Russ and Bubba walked back into the kitchen.

"Can you take us to the place where they took y'all in the woods?" Russ asked Nickie.

"I can and will but you got to help me do something first."

"Damn, what?"

"Before Hugh Jack died, he gave me two pieces of paper. One had the instructions for our meeting at the warehouse. The other was a list of all the hiding places he kept all his money, I need you to help me get it. He said I could have it."

"Oh sweetie, I don't know how to tell you this but Hugh Jack was broke. He didn't have any money," Jaimey said as she walked toward Nickie to hug her.

"The McCowan brothers got the suitcase of bones plus four duffle bags full of cash," Nickie said, full of confidence and knowledge she was sure of.

"How do you know for sure, Nickie?" Bubba asked, still uncertain. Years of gossip and speculation about Hugh Jack's financial condition told him something else entirely.

"Before he died, I found the secret wall at his barn and saw the money. I stole a roll of it. The money was real."

"What secret wall? I used to own that barn, sold it to Hugh Jack ... it didn't have a secret wall," Bubba stated, his face contorted in confusion.

"It was in the tack room, under the stair case."

"There wasn't a wall there when I owned it. Damn."

"Okay, let's go, and as soon as we're done, you show us where the McCowan brothers took you. Deal?" Russ asked, sticking his hand out toward Nickie.

Nickie nodded as she placed the last dripping bite of her concoction in her mouth.

CHAPTER THIRTY-ONE

Huny woke to sunshine piercing the window. Its tentacles reached through the tiny crack between the bottom of the shade and the window sill. She swiped at the sweat under her eyes. Her body pinned to the mattress by Bandit's nude form on top of her. When they arrived at the hotel, he collapsed after using his last bit of energy, remaining unable to move throughout the night.

"Get your ass off of me. We've got to get back to Lewiston for that singin' tonight."

Bandit groaned and slowly rolled off her onto his side of the bed, rubbing his temples and eyes.

"What time is it?"

"Time for you to get your ass up and get dressed. You need a shower, too. You smell like beer, body odor, and nasty women."

"You're the only nasty woman I've been with."

Huny slapped Bandit across the mouth and rolled over onto him straddling him, pounding on his chest playfully.

She bent down to kiss him and rose like a cork shooting from a champagne bottle.

"Go take a damn shower. Damn, you smell like shit."

Bandit stood nude, unfazed as Turtle walked through the door that connected their rooms.

"I'm goin' back tonight to kick that man's ass … look for that woman, too. The more I think about it, they set me up. They were in on it together. Y'all want to come along?"

"We got a singin' tonight, back outside a Lewiston," Huny said, holding a sheet around her shoulders.

"Y'all got any weed?" Turtle asked, knowing they did. "If you got some rolled, give me five joints."

"I don't, but I'll roll 'em for ya' real quick," Bandit said as he threw on some pants and pulled a Frisbee and bag of weed from his backpack. He sat on the bed, sprinkling pot on the papers, rolling them tight, licking the edge, and twisting the ends.

Bandit finished the joints and handed them to Turtle. Turtle gave him a twenty-dollar bill.

"Thank you. I'll be here for a few days if y'all want to come back. That bar is full of college kids who want weed. You should be able to make some good cash. I saw some good dice games goin' on, too, Bandit. Let me know, and I'll keep your room for y'all."

"Huny, Huny," Bandit shouted toward the bathroom. "You want to come back tomorrow night and go back to the bar, sell some more pot?"

"Sounds good to me," Huny said. Bandit heard the shower curtain rings move across the rod as she closed it.

"I'll keep the same room. See y'all later," Turtle said as he slid the joints into his cigarette pack and closed the door between them.

Bandit ran into the bathroom to join Huny in the shower.

CHAPTER THIRTY-TWO

Nickie sat sandwiched between Bubba and Russ on the front seat of Bubba's truck as they made their way toward Hugh Jack's house. She rested her head on Russ's shoulder as they traveled the several miles into the countryside. The season's last rolls of hay lined the roadside, leading them toward Hugh Jack's, just as bread crumbs led Hansel and Gretel toward the witch's house.

It was as if the brothers Grimm were aiding them in their journey toward riches, leading them toward a dark house in the middle of a dark pasture, and toward the cannibalistic witch that would fatten them up in hopes of eating all three.

They passed the last hay roll before the dark house came into sight. The moon and sun passed each other as the light ended. The day burned off as the slinking yellow orb slowly turned black, as if soot enveloped the burning sun.

"You sure Sheila is still in jail, Bubba," Russ asked as he stared toward the house, looking for signs of life.

"Yep. Talked to Gentry up at the jail just before we left. Shouldn't be anyone out here," Bubba said.

"Make one pass-by before we pull up in there," Russ said as he waved them on down the road.

Bubba did and soon turned around in the next driveway down the road and headed back toward the house.

Bubba reached the drive and turned into the driveway. Bumping their way over the cattle gap, his shocks proved their worth.

"Cut your lights and pull around to the back," Russ said as he turned to look behind them, making sure he saw no movement.

The three stood at the rear of the truck, each grabbing their own flashlight.

"You got the list?" Bubba asked.

"Yep," Nickie said with a lift in her voice, excited to finally be there.

She pulled out the list as they all huddled together, shining their lights on the paper.

"Let's start in the garage and move inside, then out to the pool house and the barn," Russ said, ready to be through with the treasure hunt and begin the bone hunt.

After several attempts to gain access to the house's interior, they finally found a small window that had been left unlocked. Bubba and Russ picked Nickie up and guided her head-first into the garage. She was able to land on stacked boxes that crushed under her weight and ease her way to the floor. She hurried to the side door and unlocked it. Russ and Bubba made their way in, and Russ tried the door to the house. It was unlocked. They were in.

"There is no pipe in this garage," Russ said, still impatient, feeling as if he was wasting time on an errand that would pay no dividends.

"Pipes going to be in the wall, Russ," Bubba said as he looked at him, slowly shaking his head.

Bubba eyed a long row of cabinets on the far wall and started opening doors. As he came to the next to the last one, he shined his light on a large white PVC pipe. It extended from the ceiling into the cabinet.

"Here we go," Bubba said, calling Nickie and Russ to him.

They all stood shining their light on the pipe looking at each other. Bubba took an umbrella leaning against the end of the cabinet and tapped the bottom of the pipe. It moved slightly.

"Well, that's not a real plumbing pipe," Bubba said as he took the "hook" end of the umbrella, moved it behind the pipe, and pulled it away from the back wall. The pipe slid out of the cabinet. Bubba stood one end up as a hissing sound made its way toward the bottom. Cash stacked in plastic bags slinked out like sludge from an oil derrick.

Bubba, Russ, and Nickie all stood staring at each other, shocked at what they saw, exchanging their gaze between each other and the cash that lay in heaps before them.

"I thought Hugh Jack was broke," Russ said, staring in amazement at Bubba.

"Hell, I did too. He did a hell of an acting job, fooled everybody ... shit," Bubba said, as he picked up one of the bags of green cash.

"What are we going to put this in," Nickie asked, unsure of what to do.

"Put it back in the pipe," Bubba said, realizing they already had a way to carry the cash.

They did, and Bubba and Russ picked up each end and placed it in the back of Bubba's truck.

"Okay, what's next," Russ asked, rubbing his hands

together now more in tune with the treasure hunt than before.

"It says 'false end on the bookcase,' but it don't say where," Nickie said, as she followed Russ into the house.

There were a set of bookcases in the den and a large one in Hugh Jack's study.

"It's got to be in here," Bubba said, referring to the study.

A bookshelf stretched from wall to wall and ceiling to floor behind Hugh Jack's desk. In the center was a gun safe that held twelve of Europe's finest shotguns. A long line of old encyclopedias stood like soldiers at attention on the right side of the row of guns.

Nickie bent down and pulled out two long drawers that were the same length as the gun cabinet. They each held vintage copies of *Playboy Magazines* from the seventies and early eighties.

"Damn," Bubba said as he bent down and picked up one from nineteen seventy-six. "I remember this one."

A brunette in a sheer dress graced the cover. She stood in front of the American flag. "Happy Birthday, America" was written in a banner at the bottom.

"Jayne Mansfield. Hmm I'm keeping this one," Bubba said, as he stuck the magazine in the waist of his pants.

"Can we please get back to the search?" Russ asked, half laughing at Bubba.

"It says, 'bookcase false end,'" Nickie read out loud again.

"The only end is each side of the gun safe," Bubba said as he stared at Russ.

They both opened the safe and began taking guns out of their resting places and placed them on the desk. They poked and prodded the skinny walls, but felt nothing give way.

Bubba rubbed his hands along the side of the gun safe and over three small medallions. As he did, the center one moved. Bubba rolled the medallion back and exposed a key hole.

"Here we go," Bubba said. "Need a key though."

Nickie opened up the center drawer of the desk and began to rifle through various papers, paperclips, rubber bands, and a variety of pocket knives. She accidentally moved the wooden tray that held two pearl-handled pens and picked it up. Two identical keys were taped to the drawer.

"Here!"

She separated the keys and handed them to Bubba. He fit one in the right-side keyhole and turned it. He pulled out a tray exposing rows of cash wrapped in plastic bags.

Bubba pulled out the tray and dumped it on the couch. He immediately moved to the other side, using the other key and slid out another row of wrapped cash.

"Damn!" Russ said, "I'm just not believing this. We all thought he was flat broke."

"I need something to pour this in," Bubba said as he placed the second drawer of cash on Hugh Jack's desk. "Look in that closet."

Nickie opened the door to the small coat closet she stood beside. Inside under a shelf were three large suitcases matching the ones containing both sets of remains. Seeing this intensified Russ's fervor to finish the cash grab so they could get to the McCowan compound early the next morning.

The cash from the gun safe filled up all of one suitcase and half of the second.

"Okay, where to next," Russ asked.

"Pool house and then the barn," Nickie said, as she helped Russ and Bubba replace everything as they found it.

They looked around the room making sure everything was in place and headed outside to the pool house. Once inside, they located the air vent, removed the filter, and shined a light inside, revealing a suitcase that just fit through the opening. Nickie quickly opened it and found stacks of one-hundred-dollar bills lined neatly in rows, filling the suitcase's interior.

Bubba and Russ loaded the suitcases in the bed of the truck and drove the short distance to the barn that sat roughly two-hundred yards from the house. Once there, Russ got out and opened the two large double doors allowing Bubba to drive right into the barn. Once in, he closed the doors since it was nearer the road. Nickie turned on her flashlight and read the instructions in Hugh Jack's handwriting. Tears welled in her eyes. *The fact that his last wish on earth was for me to have this money must have meant he cared for me.*

She paused, reflecting on the love he demonstrated toward her in his last moments. In such a short time she had been something different to him, something that no other woman or young girl had ever been, someone he respected and felt compassion for.

She wiped the tear meandering its way down her cheek and read the instructions. She moved the flashlight toward the back of the barn on the right side. Two horse stables stood beside each other. As they approached them, they noted stacks of legal sized banker's boxes. Various labels were affixed to the outside, mainly tax forms going back to the late seventies through the end of the eighties.

"Three loose boards under the file boxes in horse stall on far end," Nickie read out loud.

All three of them began moving the boxes from the far end of the wall until they noticed a couple of the loose boards move. Removing the boards, they pulled out ten military grade ammo boxes. Bubba struggled, extracting them from their hiding place and finally handed the last one to Nickie. The weight was too much for her, and she was forced to set it down. She opened the last one, revealing gold coins filled to the top, almost overflowing.

"How in the hell are you going to manage all of this cash and gold?" Russ asked Nickie, his eyes wide, a seemingly gold glow filling the barn.

"Well for starters, I'm splitting it with y'all. It's gonna be hard to carry around. Hell, it's all goin' to be hard to carry around."

Russ and Bubba loaded the last of the gold into the truck as Nickie replaced the loose boards and stacked the boxes back as they were, trying hard to leave no trace they were ever there. With three boxes left, Nickie struggled as she lifted a box almost above her head. She lost her grip, spilling the contents onto the floor.

She grabbed the mini light and stuck the end in her mouth to free up her hands. As she bent down to refill the box, she gasped and retreated toward Bubba and Russ. Frantically crying, hyperventilating, and unable to catch her breath, her eyes were wide with fear. She was unable to speak, but simply pointed toward the mess.

Bubba moved his light toward the spilled box and could only see papers and photos. He moved toward it for closer inspection. As he did, his eyes focused, and he gushed in horror.

"Dear God," he said, covering his mouth, trying to keep his last meal from winding up on the floor.

He moved back toward Nickie and joined her on the floor. Her inability to talk now morphed into a low moaning cry of heartache and pain—a cry that seemed to Nickie to be never ending. Bubba wrapped her in his arms and held her tight.

Russ looked at the two of them and then toward the box.

"Is there a body part or something?" he asked, thinking that could be the only explanation for their reaction.

Russ looked into Bubba's eyes, and he could only muster a slow side-to-side movement of his head. Bubba's eyes pained for Nickie. Whatever she saw that created this reaction was real to her, and that's all he needed to know.

Nickie sprang up and moved around the barn, shaking her hands as if she didn't know what to do or where to go. She felt like she just had to get out of the barn and away from that box.

Russ carefully observed this sudden burst of emotion from both Bubba and Nickie and cautiously walked toward contents that now lay scattered.

VHS tapes littered the floor. Written in black marker were labels that would bring any normal man to his knees. "*Under ten, girls and boys*" was written on one. "*Blonde fourteen*" was written on another. Thick stacks of photos fanned the floor, young girls in various stages of undress performing acts that would bring tears to any real man's eyes. Russ quickly gathered the photos in a clump when a wallet fell back to the floor. It fell open, revealing a yellowed photo of a scruffy looking man on a driver's license. The person's name, Danny Williams, and his address in Biloxi, Mississippi, glared at Russ.

Russ could hear Bubba consoling Nickie, telling her it would be okay. He picked up one more stack of papers and a small plastic card fell to the floor. He picked it up, turned it over, and immediately threw it back down.

He fell back against the barn wall, looking at Bubba, an expanse of time suddenly evident in his eyes. He picked the card back up and cradled it in his hands. He had not seen this person in the photo for years. The hardened exterior in the photo had now given way to the softness that her re-discovered grace and gentility bore ... the life of a doctor's wife whose only current worry was what time she would play tennis and how many laps she would swim each morning. The once hard lines in her face created by worry over a drunk, abusive husband and how she would care for a young teenage son were now eliminated by living a life she should have always lived.

Bubba left Nickie's side as she started to calm and made his way to Russ.

"Man, what is it?"

Russ simply opened his hands, uncovering the card, and gave it to Bubba. He looked at the square plastic card and then back at Russ. His face unknowing, confused, uncertain of what he was seeing.

"Jaimey?" Was all he could muster, his voice cracking.

He looked back at Nickie and then at Jaimey's driver's license and moved toward her. He showed her the license, and she looked away screaming, "No!" at the same time.

"It's okay, I promise. Just look," Bubba said as he moved back to Nickie's side and placed his arm around her again.

He showed her the license, and her face contorted into a quiet cry. She slowly reached out, taking the picture of Jaimey and looked at it, working her hand over her photo.

She then held the license to her heart and closed her eyes, finding comfort as if she were near her at that moment.

Russ stood quickly as if he had a mission to complete and took a deep breath. He put the contents back into the box and placed the lid on it.

"*Lewiston Inn Crime*" was written on the outside of the box.

"Bubba, look at this. What in the hell?"

"Hugh Jack used to own the Lewiston Inn back in the eighties," Bubba said.

"Why in the hell is my momma's driver license in here? Nickie, do you know?"

Nickie just shook her head, her eyes a watery red.

Russ picked up the box and loaded it in the back of the truck. As he walked back over to the remaining boxes, he turned, alerted.

"Did y'all hear that?" asked Russ.

"Turn the flashlights off," Bubba instructed, as he did the same.

The rusted creak of shocks moving slowly over the front cattle gap perked up Russ's ears as he and Bubba made their way to the barn's double doors and looked through a large crack.

A suburban slowly made its way toward the house. The small round glow of cigarettes flickered inside, like lighting bugs in a fogging machine, as billows of smoke, flowed in plumes, from its interior.

"That's Red's Suburban," Bubba whispered to Russ as if the occupants in the truck one hundred yards away could hear their conversation in the barn.

"You think he's out here doing the same thing we're doing?" asked Russ.

"I'm sure. He probably had a hand in where a lot of this

money came from," Bubba said as he looked back at Nickie who was still holding Jaimey's picture, staring at it.

"Should we wait them out or try to get the hell out of here while we have a little head start on them?" Bubba asked, as he watched the tail lights disappear behind the house, just as theirs had done only hours earlier.

"Let's go, but give them time to get in the house," Russ said, making his way back to Nickie.

He stood her up and helped her into the backseat of the truck. He moved the box into the truck cab and secured everything in the back for a fast escape.

"Okay Russ, I'm keeping the lights off. Open the doors and I'll back out. Be sure to close them behind us. I'm not hitting the brakes, so the lights don't come on. I'll just back out slowly so you jump in when you can. Let's get the hell out of here."

Russ opened both doors, and as soon as the front tires cleared, he closed them and latched them together, and ran toward the truck. Bubba threw the truck in neutral and coasted. As soon as Russ opened the door and jumped in, Bubba hit the brakes and put the truck in drive.

A distant voice shouted, "Someone's at the barn," and Bubba floored it, bouncing the truck across the cattle gap, flying over the round iron bars, vibrating the bed's contents. Metal on metal reverberated throughout the dark quiet night.

"Take a right!" Russ shouted as Bubba steered the truck to the right.

Nickie stared into the blackness behind them and saw lights blink on and dance as if someone had just jumped into the Suburban.

"Left, now."

Bubba turned left and floored it. The smoky haze of two headlights bounced over the cattle gap.

"Get down here and take your next right. You know where I'm goin?"

"Warner's?"

"Yep, you got it."

Bubba took the right, quickly, and floored it again. He slowed as they rounded a sharp curve and sped up again as the road straightened and became flat.

"The moon's full. Turn your lights out. Turn the cab lights down, too." Russ barked instructions, speeding on adrenaline.

Bubba slowed and veered onto a gravel road that cut through to the bypass. He turned his lights back on, crossing the highway and continuing onto the gravel road on the opposite side. Turning his lights back off, he soon slowed as Russ jumped out and pulled a halo of barbed wired from atop a post and slid the makeshift gate out of Bubba's way. Bubba drove through. Russ replaced the barbed wire, jumped back in the truck, and they made their way through the pasture, and backed into a hay shed.

Russ looked back at Nickie who still stared at Jaimey's photo. She stared as if it made her forget what she had just seen ... the pictures, the tapes, but mainly, Danny Williams face.

CHAPTER THIRTY-THREE

Turtle arrived at The South Shall Rise Again bar and social club" early. He felt the stares from the two gorillas, on either side of him, as he walked through the door. A crew of college boys swarmed around a pool table, drinking longnecks and holding their crotches as if they were about to wet their pants; they looked like they had skipped class and had been there most of the afternoon. They were each dressed like leftover relics from an Ivy League sailing club. Their polo shirts, khaki pants, and top sider shoes gave a stark contrast to the overalls and welding caps worn by those lingering around the pool table next to them.

Turtle sat at the bar, ordered a longneck Budweiser, and lit a cigarette. He watched as the welders, pipe fitters, brick layers, and pulpwood haulers became increasingly impatient with the soft frat boys who looked like they had never done a hard day's work in their lives. A man in a welder's hat chased balls around a table, filling the rack. His stained hands bore fresh cuts, burns and blisters from heating and forming metal. He picked up a cue and slid it over the blisters refusing to wince, refusing to show the pain.

He saw them looking toward the young boys with contempt in their eyes. He could hear their muffled murmurs and sparse words describing how soft they were, how badly they played, and how they dressed. Their words perked the eyelids of the boys... words that made them congregate in small patches and whisper.

Turtle nursed his beer, careful not to let his drinking become too much. He didn't think about Peat until he got drunk, and then those demons bombarded his soul, clogged his memory with nothing but that stupid quick decision, that stupid *selfish* decision that made his own soul ache for redemption.

When he thought about it, it made him want to fight. He needed physical pain to make the spiritual pain go away. He wondered to himself if that was why he was there tonight, in hopes of having the pain beat out of him, or was it pride? *Nobody whipped Turtle McCowan's ass and got away with it. Peat couldn't help the way he was; he couldn't help being slow. He couldn't help it, and I put an arrow through his heart for it,* Turtle thought quietly, his mind bouncing back and forth between Peat and his current predicament. He took a long, hard pull from his beer and rubbed the whiskers on his chin, more nervous than contemplative.

He turned the bottle up and drained it, then turned to the bartender and motioned for another. The pool tables began to fill as another workday drew to an end. The waitresses turned toward the bar as they walked by, getting a squirt across their ample breasts, wetting their wifebeaters in hopes of increasing their chances of better tips.

A loud static screech sounded as Rex plugged in his electric guitar and took his place behind his cage. On a nail, he replaced one end of a large pair of ladies' underwear that had fallen behind him. Dollar bills with messages and phone numbers written by desperate women and adoring fans were rolled up and stuck in the chicken wire in hopes that Rex would one day write a song about them or invite them to one of the shacks in the back.

As he continued watching the door for his "date" to arrive, Turtle saw a woman, wearing shorts with panty hose and white cowboy boots, walk through the door as if she owned the place. Her shirt was tight across her breasts, buttons holding on by the grace the struggling thread allowed them. Her hair was teased and sprayed, standing high. She still swore by the Maybelline blue eye shadow, Misty Morning, that she had used since seventy-five. She replaced what the years had stolen with padding on her rear, but she still knew how to make it work for her. It moved in a rhythm the younger girls knew nothing of, a rhythm created from love and experience, the same rhythm that matched the movement of her jaw as it chewed and popped a piece of spearmint. Her bright red painted lips were naturally thick and healthy, the portion just under her nose, wrinkled from smoking. A thumb and index finger found the corners of her mouth wiping away the excess.

She walked over to Rex and kissed him through the chicken wire. As if that were his cue, his right hand strummed the Les Paul as his fingers on the left tore down the neck. He played it as if it was on fire, and he convulsed as he sang the first line.

Hey little momma lookin' so hot ...

Rex sang at a pace the country boys found hard to keep up with, but the college boys loved. The faster and dirtier, the better for them. The blue-eyed woman started dancing by herself, moving her padded rear to the rhythm, and was soon joined by a pack of horny fraternity boys and men in overalls. The gorillas quickly moved in as the competition to win her attention erupted in pushing and the poking out of chests and spitting and cussing and poking of fingers.

Turtle watched the door, still waiting for his "date" from the previous night, as two boys were thrown through it.

CHAPTER THIRTY-FOUR

The hay barn was pitch black, even the light from the full moon couldn't penetrate the darkness, blocked by the bales surrounding them. They planned to remain there until morning, just to be sure, and then they would load a few hay bales in the truck bed, cover the cash, and head home.

"Are you okay?" Russ asked Nickie after a long, unsettling silence.

"Why does he have that box in his barn? How is that man's identification card in that box, and why is Jaimey's in there?"

"Can I ask you a question?" Russ asked respectfully.

"Yes ... that's the man. That's the man that held me for a year when I was six years old and tore me apart. That's the man that sold me to other men who tore me apart. That's the man who took those pictures and videos of me that tears me apart every day still. Is that what you wanted to know?"

"Yes."

"Why does Hugh Jack have what's in that box?" Nickie asked again, looking for answers.

"You know, Hugh Jack used to own the Lewiston Inn in the seventies and eighties. My guess is that would be his only connection. According to what's written on the box, there was some crime committed, looks like," Bubba said.

Russ heard the words "crime committed" and started putting the information he had quickly learned together. Crime, his mother's I.D., Danny Williams I.D., the pictures. He thought back to the night he killed his father and buried him and told Jaimey. She was so understanding, relieved almost.

He quickly put those thoughts out of his head. *There is no way that could have happened. She would not have been working at the Lewiston Inn. She had given that life up when we moved. The coincidence with Danny Williams being in Lewiston. How did he get here and why? Jaimey is the only reason he would have been in Lewiston. She was the only connection.*

Russ's thoughts ran through his head like a spastic squirrel looking for food when his eye caught a glimpse of a light.

"Oh shit," Russ said.

Bubba and Nickie sat up straighter in their seats, their hearts racing, unable to see anything.

"Don't turn anything on, don't open a door, be still," Bubba whispered, now seeing a brake light flash.

"They're just sitting there, not moving."

Several minutes passed with nothing happening. The car remained in one location, the motor still running.

"Stay right here. Don't move, hear me," Russ said as he lowered his window and slinked out of it headfirst, falling to the ground on his hands.

Russ eased his way through the tall grass, darting

behind round bales of hay for cover until he was able to get near the edge of the road. He slowly peered around a hay bale until he could make out a Camaro. Through the fogged windows he could make out movement and hear joyous shrieks and low moans emanating from inside.

Russ turned away and rested his back against the hay bale, finally letting out air he had been holding since his stalk began.

He made his way back to the hay barn and crawled back through the window just to be safe.

"What was it," Nickie asked nervously.

"Two kids making out. I think we're fine but I think we should wait here until morning. Let's try to get some sleep."

Russ's mind began wandering, thinking again about his mother and the hotel and Danny Williams. He looked back at Nickie and then at Bubba. They were both asleep.

Night

itch-black was framed by the glow of gold grass swaying in a windless night. The blackness remained empty until a white skull slowly rose from its floor eventually revealing its full skeletal form. It walked in a broken gait toward him and stopped, staring into the blackness. The gold grass waving through the transparent form between bones that now bent down and extended a hand, pulling from the grass another form, same as him, as if pulling it from a grave. They stood beside each other almost identical in form, angry. Above each of their skulls was a sign. "Beau Chene Country Club," was above the one on the left. The other flashed in neon, "The Lewiston Inn." The two forms stared at Russ, the black depths of their eye sockets piercing his eyes until finally the one on the left raised a hand with an extended finger and pointed at him.

"You brought death," it said.

The other spoke after the first.

"Your mother brought death."

Russ woke, his mouth dry, sweating. His breathing started to slow and he sat straight up. He squinted as he stared at the sharp beams of the rising sun, cresting a hill, poking through the tree line. Cows stood before him in a long row, their mouths moving in a circular motion chewing hay, staring blankly at him. Another uneasy morning had come.

CHAPTER THIRTY-FIVE

Turtle stared at the blue-eyed woman's waist. She looked like she borrowed her whole body from Dolly Parton. Her waist was tiny, but made to look even smaller as it was sheltered by her large breasts. The Gogo shorts from the previous night maintained their short length, only changing in color. Last night's silver shorts were now satin pink and had "Juicy" written across the rear.

The pantyhose she wore on her legs came from a small egg. They smoothed her wrinkles and assisted at holding gravity at bay. They provided a year-long tan and hid the varicose veins now turning her legs a soft purple from her sixty-three years.

She moved beside Turtle and propped herself on the bar on both elbows and reached between her breasts, extracting a single tube of lipstick. She adjusted her wig purchased in eighty-three in Memphis for her second honeymoon. She applied the bright red color to her lips, asked Turtle where he was from, and ordered a beer all at the same time.

"Mississippi," he answered as he turned toward her.

She reversed the roll, closed it, and slid the tube back in her dark crevasse, slowly attempting to pull Turtle's eyes toward her cleavage.

"Private Collection?" Turtle asked as he leaned a little closer, filling his nose with her heavy perfume.

"Naw honey, it's a knock off from Wal-Mart. Good nose, though."

Turtle tipped his drink toward her.

"Just so we're straight, I ain't flirtin' with you. Rex is my man; just makin' conversation."

"Understood, I'll buy you a beer anyway."

"Hell Sweetie, I get my drinks free, one of the perks from sleepin' with the owner. Whatcha drinkin'?"

"Bud in a bottle, thank you."

"Nasty cut you got there hun, nice and fresh. What happened?"

"Compliments of one of your customers from last night."

"Now look, you see those two at the door right there?" the blue-eyed woman asked, pointing a well-manicured red nail toward the two gorillas. "They won't tolerate any shit; both sides of your face will match after the night is over if you start something."

"Well, they tolerated it last night while I got my ass kicked."

"Good point, I'd just be sure to take it outside if I was you though."

"Understood and thank you," Turtle said as he tipped his free beer toward the blue-eyed woman.

She left Turtle and walked back toward the cage where Rex sat on his barstool, singing a slow song he dedicated to her. She opened the chicken wire gate and joined him inside, dancing around Rex, swaying behind him with her arms wrapped around his neck.

Turtle trained his eye back on the door, watching, trying to remember what the woman looked like from two nights ago. It was all such a blur; the pain in his head would not allow the vison of her to be clear in his mind. He hoped he would just know her as soon as he saw her.

What looked like regulars wearing denim and dirt started flowing in, and soon the clinking of beer bottles and aluminum caps being pried off filled the air around him. A sober, well-behaved group of fraternity brothers filed through the door, replacing their I.D.'s in their billfolds. They all raced toward the bar, each ordering buckets of beers and exchanging dollar bills for quarters to play pool.

A quick, light ruckus broke out as the overzealous frat boys moved in too quickly on a pool table already occupied by men who had been working that day. Chests poked out and fingers pointed. It lasted only a short time as one of the young boys realized the finger was being pointed back from well above him. His soberness allowed the good decision to quickly absorb his pride and move on.

Turtle tipped his bottle up high, extracting the last drop of Budweiser, and turned to the bartender to order another. As he reached into his pocket and pulled out a roll of cash, he felt a hand sweep across his shoulders. Long fingernails tickled just under his left ear. He peeled a ten from the top, told the bartender to keep the change, and felt breathing in his ear.

"Buy a girl a drink?"

Bingo. He turned toward the voice staring at a redhead with emerald green eyes and immediately fell in love.

Turtle looked the woman up and down. Tight black leather pants tucked into cowboy boots covered with rhinestones hugged her perfect figure, set off by a hot pink tank top that simply read "Guess" across the front. She looked like a leftover from a Dallas rerun, and Turtle fancied himself an oil man. His chest poked out and his smile broadened.

"Are those your real eyes," Turtle asked, mesmerized by their color.

"As real as it gets sugar," the woman said slowly and deliberately.

"My name's Penny. What's yours?"

"Turtle."

"That's a new one, I've heard of a Rabbit and a Rooster before, but Turtle's a new one. How in the world did you get a name like Turtle?"

"You know, you sure are pretty," Turtle said as he peered into the green abyss of her eyes, becoming lost in them. The events of the night he was beaten drained from his memory with every sweet syllable she whispered in his ear. The night wore on. Beer after beer followed by tequila shots flowed down their throats as smooth as a George Jones song.

Turtle's need to feel pain and erase Peat from his mind was being replaced with the numbness the alcohol provided. With every purchase and no bar tab, the rubber band popped over and over again. The green eyes focused on the roll every time Turtle extracted it from his front pocket. She smiled more broadly, licked her lips at him, and rubbed his chest.

Bandit and Huny returned as promised. They sat against the wall across from Turtle watching intently for signs of trouble. Watching for someone lurking, waiting to pounce, waiting to follow Turtle outside, jump him, and take the roll in his pocket.

"This plan ain't thought out well," Bandit whispered to Huny. "He's drunk off his ass, and I'm too old to fight anybody off. What the hell are we supposed to do if something happens?"

"Go get his keys, he's about ready to go anyway," Huny said as she motioned toward Turtle.

Bandit walked over to Turtle, whispered something in his ear, and took the keys from his hand. Huny walked the two to the door and stood with them, staring at the bouncers, waiting on the Corvette to appear at the front door. Turtle and Penny could not take their eyes off each other.

All three stood at the door, resembling a bride and groom and matron of honor as Rex began singing a song about sex in the back of a sixty-four Studebaker truck. The camaraderie of young men grew louder as a black ball sunk into a corner hole and the wedding party made it out of the door. Huny slid the ginger beauty into the passenger's seat while Bandit held the door for Turtle on the driver's side.

"We'll stay here and give y'all time before we head back," Bandit said, winking at Turtle.

"Thank you, buddy," Turtle said as he patted Bandit on the arm.

As they pulled away Penny immediately attached herself like glue to Turtle's side, wrapping her arms around his and nibbling on his ear.

"You gon' have to stop that or we ain't gon' make it back to the hotel."

"Where are we going anyway?"

"Southaven. I got a real nice room at the Hampton Inn."

"Let's stop by the liquor store so we can keep this party goin'," Penny said as she moved her hand down along the inside of Turtle's thigh.

Turtle pulled into the ABC Package store and asked Penny what she wanted.

"Wine, wine, and more wine," she said, almost shouting and almost drunk.

Turtle disappeared into the store as Penny watched in the rearview mirror for the headlights of the SUV. Soon the lights appeared and pulled off to the side of the parking lot. Turtle returned with two brown paper bags and handed them to Penny to hold as they drove right beside the SUV on their way out of the parking lot and onto the street. Penny glanced at the driver and returned her attention toward Turtle and the wine.

"You got a corkscrew hun?"

"Not in here," Turtle said, half laughing. "Hell, we don't need to get arrested before we get to the hotel."

"We sure don't, because I'm fixin' to turn your world upside down sugar," Penny said, as she licked Turtle's cheek.

Turtle smiled and stared at her, disbelieving his good fortune. He looked her up and down, imagining her naked and stepped on the accelerator, his speed now matching his heart rate.

They pulled into the hotel parking lot and jumped out. They each held a bottle as they made their way toward number sixteen on the bottom floor. Once inside, Penny asked for the corkscrew while Turtle ducked into the bathroom.

Penny quickly popped the cork, poured a glass for Turtle, unfolded the waxed paper, and stirred the crushed white powder into Turtle's wine.

"Drink up," she said as she handed him the glass with one hand, while placing her other one on his crotch.

He drank up quickly and downed it all so he could be through with that and get on to the business at hand.

Penny pushed him down on the bed and slowly undressed him. He lay on the bed, nude, spread-eagle, smiling as Penny slowly started to undress. She undressed down to her red bra and panties.

"You got any socks here?"

"In the top drawer," Turtle said, a confused frown pushing down his face.

His frown quickly turned into a devilish smile as Penny began tying his ankles to the bedpost, moving from there up to his wrists.

Penny turned to the wine and poured them both another glass emptying the last of the powder into Turtle's. She placed the two glasses down on the bedside table and crawled on top of him straddling just below his chest. She took off her bra, leaned over him and poured the wine between her breasts allowing it to trickle down into his mouth. She held his head up and poured the rest into his mouth, feeling him begin to drift away from her. His eyelids became heavy as she kissed his mouth, keeping his suspicion at bay. When he stopped returning her kiss, she slid off of him and stood above him watching for movement, but he was comatose, out for the next several hours.

She quickly dressed and began moving around the room, first picking up his pants, taking the two rolls and car keys from his two front pockets, putting them in her purse. She knelt down and looked under the bed, but the mattress sat on an enclosed box, making it impossible to slide anything underneath. She moved to the closet and opened the gold framed mirrored doors. With the exception of two Western style shirts and one pair of heavily starched Wrangler jeans, the closet was empty. The small safe door was open and empty.

She looked in the small space between one of the beds and the wall and found nothing. With as much strength as she could muster, she slid the mattress off of the empty bed only exposing an empty space full of cobwebs, dirt, and a used condom.

The only other place to look was under the bed Turtle now lay on. She stood at the base of the bed, her hands on her hips, trying to figure out if she could move him or not. She had planned on pocketing any extra cash before her accomplice could lay their hands on it.

"Some's better than none," she said out loud to herself.

She slowly poked her head out the door and motioned toward the SUV. A short, fat man scurried toward the room. Penny held her index finger to her mouth making sure he remained quiet as he made his way toward the room.

Once inside he looked at Turtle laying nude, spread-eagled and tied to each corner of the bed.

"I've looked everywhere," Penny whispered. "The only place left is under this bed he's on. You're going to have to help me move him," she said as she untied his hands and feet.

Turtle softly muttered under his breath, and the two of them froze momentarily, staring at him, watching his eyes for movement.

"You grab under his arms, and I'll get his feet," Penny said as she grabbed each leg under the knee.

"One, two, three," Penny counted, and they lifted him and threw him on the opposite bed in one motion.

They both stood bent over, resting their hands on their knees and catching their breath. Turtle turned onto his side and snored loudly.

"You get that end," Penny said. They both lifted and pushed the mattress off of its base.

"Bingo!"

As they stared at the two duffle bags and a leather suit case, they heard the adjoining room door shut. Bandit beat on the door.

"Y'all don't have too much fun in there, kids."

"Say something. Make a noise or something," Penny whispered.

"Whoohoo!"

They heard Bandit laugh and were satisfied that he was happy with the response.

Penny unzipped the larger duffle bag and saw that it was full of loose cash. They pulled the bags and the suitcase from under the bed, and slid the mattress back on the frame, straightening the bedding back on the mattress.

Penny looked out the door and noticed an opened parking spot on the opposite side of the door from Bandit and Huny's room.

"Back your car in that spot as quietly as you can."

The SUV took the spot, and the two of them moved quickly and quietly toward the rear where they placed the bags and suitcase. She poured herself into Turtle's Corvette, and they were gone.

Exhaustion danced around insomnia causing bouts of unrest.

The darkness came in spurts, a bright light bounced back and forth like a heartbeat, pulsing, moving closer and then farther away. The light barely shone until finally it grew and stood erect in its skeletal form, still. The form finally laid down on a blanket of green grass, curling itself into the fetal position, almost making itself completely square. As insomnia began beating away exhaustion, the light shone small and less bright, turning to black. His eyes opened, and the light reappeared directly above him on the ceiling. Its rays clipped with the turning of the ceiling fan.

Russ woke and lay still. He felt as if he would never see the skeleton again, as if it were gone forever, a feeling he had yet to feel.

CHAPTER THIRTY-SIX

Russ sat at the kitchen table drinking coffee, his eyes red from interrupted sleep and his attempt to rub the tired away. He rose and walked into the store room off the garage and found Nickie sitting in the center of the money, counting.

"I'm givin' you and Bubba some of this."

"Give my share to Bubba; don't want it."

"You serious? You ain't gon' take any? Who gives up free money? The IRS don't even know about this shit."

"Don't want it. I just need to find the suitcase with the remains in it. That's all I care about."

"I need a damn calculator," Nicky said, looking around her and exhausted from being up all night counting.

"So, what are you up to?"

"Four hundred and fifty thousand, give or take a couple a hundred bucks."

"Where you 'spose this money came from?"

"Nothing good, I can promise you that."

"I can buy me a house, hell two. How much does a house cost anyway?"

"I'll get you hooked up with a good financial advisor and accountant. They will be discreet and quiet. Everything will be done off the books. They can provide advice only," Russ offered. "Have you even thought about where you're going to put all this money? Hell, you can't go to a bank. This is about to be a headache."

"Hell, it can't be no more of a headache than being broke and homeless."

"Look, the money is safe here. As we agreed, you would help me find the McCowan Brothers if I helped you find the cash. I need you to take me to the place where they took you and Hugh Jack. Why don't you go take a shower and get dressed. By that time Bubba will be here, and we can leave as soon as you're ready."

Nickie stood, made her way toward the stairs to take a shower, and met Jaimey coming down. She grabbed Jaimey and hugged her quietly for several minutes and without saying a word ran up the stairs.

"What was all that about?"

"This," Russ said as he threw Jaimey's driver's license at her.

Jaimey picked up the plastic card and stared into the eyes of a person she barely knew any longer, a person she didn't want to know. She stared at a damaged woman, hardened by a life of uncertainty and abuse. Her eyes never left the photo as tears flowed into skinny streams down her cheeks.

She swiped at them.

"Where did you find this?" she asked, scared of the response.

Without saying a word, Russ threw another driver's license on the table toward her. Before she picked it up, she saw the face and then the name Danny Williams.

"These, along with various other things, including kiddie porn, were in a box labeled, "The Lewiston Inn." We found the box in Hugh Jack's barn. Bubba said he used to own The Lewiston Inn in the eighties. Why is your I.D. in the same box with Danny Williams? He's the pedophile, right, that kidnapped Nickie?"

"Yes ... he is."

"So, what was he doing in Lewiston, and why are both of your I.D.'s in the same box?"

Jaimey placed both hands on her forehead, her fingers intertwined, and looked up toward the ceiling. Her head felt as if it would split wide open. For several minutes she didn't speak.

"Can't we just forget you found this and pretend this never happened?"

"We could, but I don't think we could move on like we need to. Nickie would like to have answers."

Russ felt his heart rate increase as the possibilities started clicking through his mind.

"If it's what I think it is, it would probably be good therapy for you, and I know it would be for Nickie."

"Damn," Jaimey said. "I thought all of this was over. God, I'm tired of this. I knew this would eventually catch up with me. Sixteen years. There have been days when I didn't think about my past, but then there were others when I would worry. I knew this day was coming."

"Yeah, I know. I'm the only one who knows exactly how you feel."

"Feel about what," Jim Spencer said as he rounded the corner with a cup of coffee in his hand, starting the day in his usual upbeat manner.

Jaimey slid the two I.D.'s in the pocket of her robe.

"I am so glad you're back. We're just talking about Mom

meeting Nickie after all these years and finding the remains."

"Well, it will all be over soon, and we can get back to our normal lives. Got to get to the office," Jim said as he planted a kiss on Jaimey's lips.

"If I tell you and Nickie, that man can never know, you understand?" Jaimey asked as she watched through the window as Jim got into his car.

"I don't agree, but I do understand."

"You'll agree after I tell you my story. Is Bubba on his way?"

"Yes."

"Call him and tell him to wait about an hour, this is just between you, me, and Nickie."

"Okay."

Jaimey and Russ sat at the table in silence as Nickie made her way down the stairs. She stopped in the living room, put on her shoes, and eventually joined them in the kitchen.

"Come sit down," Jaimey said as she patted the chair next to her.

"Russ said you found a box with my I.D. in it?"

"Yes, and that bastard's I.D., too … and the pictures, and the other stuff. Why was your I.D. there?"

Jaimey let out a long, loud sigh. "The day we escaped from that trailer, do you remember asking me to go back inside and get your doll?"

Nickie jumped up and ran up the stairs. She soon came back down holding a dirty, tattered doll.

"This is Sara."

Jaimey took the doll in her hand, and the events of that day became clearer in her mind. Seeing the doll gave her a sense that what she went through was all worth it. She had kept Sara all these years. Through all of the foster homes, through all of the abuse, Nickie still had her. Jaimey recounted the day.

"When I went back inside to get Sara, there was a green duffle bag on the floor, full of money. I took it. I'm not proud of that, but I took it. Russ, we needed money so badly and we had to get out of Biloxi. I thought I had just killed a man and had to run."

"Wait, what do you mean, thought you killed him? I saw you shoot him that day; he fell down, hit his head, and looked dead," Nickie said, not quite understanding what she was hearing.

"I thought he was dead, too, but several weeks later he tracked me down here in Lewiston?"

"Here?" Nickie asked, as she sat up straighter in her chair.

"Yes, we were living with Cappy. Russ, it was the night of the Calcutta thing at the country club. Effie came to pick me up."

"Who is Effie," Nickie asked.

"She was one of the most wonderful people I have ever known. Danny Williams found out we lived in Lewiston and somehow tracked Effie to Cappy's house. He forced his way in, and we ran. We ran out of the house and hid in the woods. He hunted us down. I shot and finally killed him that night."

Jaimey watched Russ and Nickie's faces. Russ was in disbelief, and Nickie just sat with her head down, slowly crying, shaking.

"You mean before you came to the Calcutta, that night?" Russ asked.

"Yes."

"Well, what does this have to do with the motel box we found?" Nickie asked, confused.

"After I killed him, in self-defense mind you," Jaimey took a deep breath, "After I shot him, we loaded his body in his truck. We found his keys for the truck and on the ring was a room key to The Lewiston Inn. We took his body back to the inn, dragged him inside his room, and propped him up in the bed. We staged the room to look like a pissed off father had found and killed a pedophile. It must have worked. I never heard another thing until now."

Russ sat emotionless, unable or unwilling to speak.

"Why did Hugh Jack keep this all these years? How does he have these and the police don't?"

"Probably for the same reason he was blackmailing me for the bones. He's an opportunist, just waiting for information to pop up about a murder that happened in the eighties. Remember, he had evidence. Then he would try to sell the evidence for cash. It was always about the money for Hugh Jack," Russ said.

It was difficult for Nickie to listen to talk of Hugh Jack. Most of it wasn't pleasant. Most of it wasn't her experience. She would always have a love for him. She possibly saw a part of Hugh Jack that many never saw.

"So, in the span of one weekend, you and I killed two people?" Russ asked in disbelief.

"Two people that needed to be killed," Jaimey added.

Nickie stood and moved to Jaimey and hugged her. "Thank you, I'm sorry you went through all of that because of me. I always thought he died that day."

Russ stood as well, moved toward Jaimey, and did the same.

"I'm sorry you've had to live with this all these years. I

guess at the very least we can say we're survivors," Russ said, wiping away tears.

Jaimey looked at the two of them.

"Not a word about this to anyone, especially Jim. You understand?"

They both nodded their agreement.

CHAPTER THIRTY-SEVEN

Bubba blew the horn in the driveway and waited for Russ and Nickie as he sat in his baby blue Ford Bronco, a gift from Cappy.

"Where's the truck?"

"Thought it might be better to park it for a while after the other night, just in case they caught a glimpse of it."

"Good thinking."

"Okay, where to?" Bubba asked.

"Go to Hugh Jack's barn at Beau Chene so I can start from there," Nickie said, trying to remember the turn they took after leaving the barn. She remembered the Corvette and imagined following it.

"Turn left onto the bypass," Nickie said sitting in the backseat between Bubba and Russ.

"We gon' go by a place with some trucks with big poles on the back of them."

"Electric company," Russ and Bubba said simultaneously.

Passing the electric company, Nickie instructed Bubba

to turn left on the road "between two pastures with cows in them."

"Right there," Russ pointed as Bubba turned left.

"You gon' go over some railroad tracks way down here and turn off right as soon as you go over the tracks."

Bubba drove another two miles, winding his way deeper into the unknown, until he finally came to the railroad tracks. A long train full of sawdust and lumber was crossing. Bubba put the Bronco in park and waited.

As the last car passed them, Nickie adjusted herself in the back seat.

"Whoa, back up."

"I didn't see a road," Bubba said.

"It ain't no road. It's more of a pig trail."

Bubba put the Bronco in reverse, turned, and drove through a short field before he hit a small opening in the trees. They danced across the stone bottom of a trickling ford. As they came out on the other side, they drove into a small compound surrounded by shacks that were rotting and in need of paint.

Turtle shells hung from boards extended between trees. Snake skins were nailed to the side of one of the buildings. Beer cans and whisky bottles littered the ground where they parked the Bronco and stepped out. Three rusted heaps of metal, slowly being eaten by kudzu, stood in a mound.

Bubba walked to what looked like the main house and tried the door. It was open. As he walked in, turtle shells filled every space of the ceiling. The smell of musty, rotting death filled his nose. The place looked as though it had been closed up for weeks. A piece of paper with a list of numbers on it sat on the kitchen counter. Russ and Nickie entered behind Bubba as they all three fanned their noses, their faces scowling at the stench.

"Damn, this is some shit ain't it," Nickie said as she looked around the room in amazement.

"Check those two doors in the back, Bubba," Russ said, as he made his way under the shells into the den.

"Nothing back here."

"Where did they take y'all out here," Russ asked.

"Come on," Nickie said as she made her way out the door, leading them down a small trail deeper into the woods.

"They tied Hugh Jack up right there."

The structure Hugh Jack was tied to still floated between the two trees. Rope, chain, and cut zip ties dangled from them, swaying softly in the wind. The ground below was littered with apple cores that had turned brown and had been consumed by ants devouring the last of the edible morsels. Russ walked to the rope and inspected it more closely. Blood stains remained on the ends. The constant buzzing of flies was the only sound he heard. The woods around them were eerily quiet. The faint smell of rotting flesh hit all of their noses at once.

"What is that?" Bubba asked, pointing toward the pond. They all walked toward a large mound of dirt. There was a bloody arrow forced into the ground, taking the place of a headstone.

"I don't think I want to know what that is. This place smells like death. Let's get the hell out of here."

"Where to now?" Bubba asked, as they drove back up the trail, making their way back over the ford and out onto the main road.

"Let's go see if Tur... Paul and Peat's mother know where they are."

Bubba pointed the Bronco toward town and turned off the highway onto North Columbus Avenue. They drove north toward Main Street, past one antebellum house after another. The street known as Antebellum Alley held twenty-six of Lewiston's most beautiful houses.

As they neared the end of North Columbus, the largest, whitest house with the largest columns on the alley sat on the right side of the street.

Bubba turned between two live oaks that stood at the entrance of the drive leading to the house. A sign that read "Bent Oaks, circa 1860," welcomed them onto the property.

"Should we really just be going to see her without an appointment or at least calling first?" Bubba asked, feeling intimidated and uneasy.

"This woman we are about to meet moved from the shithole that we just left to this house. Consider that before you feel intimidated," Russ said. "She simply married well, that's all."

"Holy shit," Nickie said, as she stood looking up at the house's two stories.

"My God, Pamela move your ass if you want something to eat, dammit!" a loud shrill voice filled the air as Bubba, Russ, and Nickie walked toward the door.

The voice came from behind the house. As they made their way toward the sound, they saw no one.

The house was pre-Civil War and freshly painted white. The azalea bushes and crepe myrtle trees held onto their last bit of life before winter would claim them. The grass had been meticulously cut, edged, fertilized, and watered. Behind the house was a three-acre lake with a small barn and paddock areas made of stone.

Chickens moved along the ground in a jerk, pecking and digging for a morsel of grain. Their high-pitched bawking grew louder and more frequent, warning that intruders were in the yard. Two friendly German shorthair pointers greeted them. Russ extended the back of his hand to the first to arrive, and he licked it and smelled it. Satisfied they weren't a threat, they both ran toward the lake, looking for a place to jump from the pier into the water for an afternoon swim.

"Mrs. McCowan," Russ called, both hands cupped around his mouth. As he called, a peacock slowly walked up behind them from the lake, screaming, stretching its vocal cords to maximum capacity.

"Shit!" Bubba yelled, jumping and looking behind him at the same time. "I'm just waiting for Dr. Doolittle to appear any minute. I didn't know all of this was smack dab in the middle of town. I thought she got remarried. Did she keep her last name?"

"Habit, that's all I've ever called her," Russ said.

"What the hell is this place," Nickie asked.

Soon two large glass doors parted as if wind had blown them open. Shortly the doorway filled with a blonde woman in a flowing gown. A stemmed glass in one hand and a bottle to fill it in the other.

"She looks like a movie star," Nickie whispered to Bubba.

A big-bosomed woman, her breasts were lifted not by youth, and pushed together, exposing her long-freckled cleavage. Lost in her cleavage was a single strand of pearls that fell between them and disappeared within her dress. Her hair was creamy blonde, natural, without an ounce of gray and fixed large around her head. It appeared she single-handedly kept the hairspray manufacturers in business. Fake eyelashes framed her ice blue eyes. Her lips were painted a soft pink.

She was a girl from the county who, after three tries finally married well, having been brought in from the country to the big city. Her personal transition from farm girl to socialite was spotless with the exception of her speaking voice. That was one thing that didn't leave the country.

As elegant as she looked, when she opened her mouth, all pretenses had to be dropped.

She approached her guests as elegantly as Princess Grace at a red-carpet gala. She even stuck out her hand in greeting as if she were Marilyn Monroe herself; but, then, as soon as she opened her mouth, she made the trip from Hollywood to Mississippi faster than Richard Petty in the last lap at Talladega.

"How are you, ma'am?" Bubba asked, her breasts begging his attention.

"I'm Pearl Jean McCowan Stevens. So nice to meet you," she said, as she introduced herself to Bubba.

"Why, aren't you just the cutest little thang," Pearl said as she turned her attention toward Nickie. "How are y'all? I'm so glad to have y'all here. Russ, Darlin', y'all want some wine? Lord knows it's hot as hell out here."

"Well, we ju ..."

"Pamela, dammit, Y'all excuse me just a minute. Get your ass back in that pen," she said, shooing a pot belly pig back into its living quarters. "Mabel, please bring that other bottle of wine out here and some glasses."

"Pamela was Frank's last wife. She was a fat pig too."

As if she had already read Pearl's mind, Mabel had the wine uncorked and poured everybody a glass. Nickie turned hers up quickly and drained the contents in one gulp. She reached for the bottle and poured herself another glass.

"You look like you'd make a good drinkin' buddy, Sugar."

"Yes ma'am," was all Nickie could get out. She looked on Pearl with pure amazement. She was larger than life. Nickie had never met anyone quite like her before.

"Now, what can I do for y'all?"

"Well, we were wondering if you might know where we could find Turtle and Peat?" Russ asked, finishing his wine.

"Oh God, what have they done now?" Pearl asked as she poured herself more wine. "You know we don't really get along all that well. Those boys are both crazy as hell, and Peat, well he's special you know."

"We uh, Nickie here, was interested in some of that jewelry that Turtle makes," Russ said watching Nickie for her response.

"Sure thing. I saw a necklace the other day on this woman, and she told me she got it from Turtle. I got to have me one."

Russ could feel Nickie's eyes piercing the side of his head, searching for approval of her story.

"If they're not out at the old home place, I can't imagine where they'd be. Peat usually sticks pretty close to home, but when Paul goes out of town, he usually goes to a honky-tonk just over the line near Memphis. He doesn't know that I know he goes up there to sell that pot to those college kids. Thinks he's bein' smart. He's got all that money from his daddy's lawsuit burning a damn hole in his pocket."

"You don't by chance know the name of that bar do you," Bubba asked as he bent over to place a dip in his lip.

"Oh God, it's something to do with the war."

As Pearl thought, she poked her forehead with her index finger.

"Which war?" Bubba asked.

"The Civil War," she said to him as if the world had not experienced two world wars, the Korean War, and the war in Vietnam, since then.

"Confederate something. The south is in it … The South Shall Rise Again. That's it, The South Shall Rise Again bar and social club. Down the road from Southaven," she said. "But look, y'all don't have to go that far; wait right there."

Russ, Bubba and Nickie sat waiting, staring at each other, whispering, and wondering what she was doing. Soon Pearl returned with a shoebox.

"I'm glad you like them, but I personally think they look like crap."

Nickie opened the box that was filled with all types of rudimentary jewelry made from turtle shells.

"I couldn't dare take these from you. He made these 'specially for you."

"Aw shit, he gave me those for birthdays and Mother's Day because he was too cheap to go buy me something. I knew the whole time, he had a pocket full of that dope money. He's cheap like his daddy was. Now Peat's daddy spent some money on me, but not Rayford. That son of a bitch was just plain sorry and cheap as hell."

"Well, thank you so much," Nickie said as she took out a necklace and slipped it over her head.

Russ stood and thanked Pearl and leaned over to shake her hand. She stood and hugged him and kissed him on the cheek.

"Russ, tell that gorgeous mother of yours I said Hey!"

"I sure will, Ms. Pearl."

"Thank you, again," Nickie said, as she fondled the necklace.

As they rounded the corner toward the garage, they heard Pearl shout.

"Jenny, get your ass back up here right now and eat, dammit."

"Who's Jenny? Another maid?" Bubba asked.

"Her mule," Russ said, shaking his head.

"How do you know her?"

"That woman was the only person that truly accepted my mother when everyone around Lewiston found out what she had done for a living in Biloxi. All the other women looked down on her. Pearl gave her a job at her beauty parlor. If it weren't for Cappy and Pearl, no telling where we'd be right now."

CHAPTER THIRTY-EIGHT

The dark blue midnight sky encased the full yellow moon that hung just above the South Shall Rise Again bar and social club. The "social club" designation allowed them to remain a private club, which meant they could refuse service to anyone.

The bar area simply provided a front for what went on in the back. The real cash flow came from drugs and weapons. In addition, there was a row of small buildings in the back for prostitution.

Penny and her driver stood with Rex around a pool table in the room directly behind the stage surrounded by chicken wire. On the table were two duffle bags and an opened leather suitcase exposing Randy's remains.

Penny unzipped the duffle bags full of cash. Rex's eyes lit up.

"Now that's more like it," he said as he grabbed a fist full of cash and put it up to his nose and inhaled deeply.

Rex threw the cash back into the bag and told the blue-eyed woman to count it. She transferred the cash to another table that sat parallel to one surrounded by Rex and Penny and the hired help. They remained, circling the table, staring at the bones. Rex began taking the pieces out and reconstructing the skeleton on the table.

"Looks like this fella was about six feet tall, been dead a long time, maybe twenty years roughly. Not embalmed, no casket."

"How can you tell?" Penny asked, genuinely interested.

"See these places here and here," Rex asked pointing to the area around the eye sockets. "Those little ridges and rough areas are where insects have been nibbling on the bone. This fella was just dumped in the dirt."

Rex took the head and lifted it up.

"Get me a pair of pliers," he said to no one in particular.

"This fella, whoever he was, had some money," Rex said as he used the pliers to break off a gold cap and hold it up to the light.

"Put that in with the others," he said as he handed the gold tooth to the man standing next to him.

"Where was this fella?"

"Hotel in Southaven."

"How did you leave him?"

"Asleep and happy," Penny said as she smiled at her driver.

"This fella's going to want these bones back. There's a reason he has them. He'll be back lookin' for them. If he has this much cash, he's probably got more. I'll be more than happy to sell them back to him, so be on the lookout."

Penny nodded.

"You boys keep an eye out. When he comes back, he'll be looking for Penny. Don't let him get near her."

Everyone nodded in unison.

"How much we got over there?" Rex asked the blue-eyed woman who was still organizing the bills by denomination.

"I'll know shortly," The blue-eyed woman said, popping her gum.

"Here, put these back in that suitcase and put it behind my desk," Rex said to Penny.

Penny's face turned sour. She didn't want to touch the bones so she used the pliers and picked them up one by one. She dropped them in the leather suitcase, zipped it up, and placed it behind Rex's desk, out of sight.

CHAPTER THIRTY-NINE

Russ and Bubba arrived at the office the following morning. They discussed the ongoing project in the Carolinas and received updates on the smaller jobs ongoing from their project managers.

Once satisfied the business was running as smoothly as it could without them, they both headed to Beau Chene to check on the number ten green.

Dotted all over the course were the usual early morning crews of older retired men who tried to get a round in while the sun still hid behind sparse clouds before the heat set in for the day.

A trail of laughter slowly dissolved into the morning breeze. The groans of nearly successful putts sounded around the course as a litany of curse words followed the ball's trajectory away from the hole.

"I miss this, Bubba."

"Miss what?"

"I miss coming to a golf course when the only thing on my mind is golf. Then goin' home and playing with Will and maybe getting lucky later that night with Angie. It was just so simple. I miss the simplicity, and I miss playing. It's not just what's going on right now, but all the time. I just miss playing golf without a worry. Of course, there has only been a short span of time in my life when it seemed I had no worries, but it did make an impression."

"We'll get back there, buddy. Let's get this thing behind us, finish these projects we're working on, and then you can slow down a little. Hell, when we go back to South Carolina you should stay a couple of extra weeks and play up there."

"No, Beau Chene. I want to come play Beau Chene, with these old men and the boys... out here, on my home course. You know, a lot of these guys remember Cappy. Played with him. I want to be with them and talk about Cappy, and I want you there, too, Bubba. I just want to go back to a place when I was so happy playing with you and Cappy and the boys. I want to see Curtis and Duckhead and Fatboy, all of them."

"Hey tell you what. Let's have our own little Cappy memorial tournament, Thursday through Sunday when this is all over. Just us and the boys," Bubba said as he grabbed Russ's head and put him in a playful headlock.

They arrived at the number ten fairway, drove past the caution tape and up the dogleg toward the green. Jose' was just making the final cut on the green. The grass was lush and dark from fertilizer.

"Just about through Jose'?" Russ asked as he got out of the golf cart and walked toward him. "The green looks a little larger."

"It is. I moved the retaining wall back a little farther and added something. I hope you don't mind."

Jose' led Russ and Bubba to the front of the green and then walked them down the hill along a newly built stairway to the bottom.

"Sand Trap! That's the only one on the whole course. Why didn't we think of that, Bubba?"

"This way, Mister Russ. The sand will help the water drain and save the balls from rolling into the woods."

"Damn, Jose', you're going to be taking over my job before much longer. The retaining wall looks great, too. Good job. I wish I had a sand wedge."

"Tirame un palo de golf!" Jose shouted toward the top of the green. Soon a sand wedge flew through the air toward him. He caught it and handed it to Russ.

"I need a ball, too."

Bubba bounded back to the golf cart and threw one down to Russ. Russ fondled the ball on the sand with the wedge, took a couple of practice swings and set his feet, burying them firmly in the sand.

He turned the wedge flat against the sand and exchanged glances with the top of the flag and the ball in front of him, then took a full swing. The sand pushed out of the trap and onto the green. The ball rolled a foot from the flag.

"Still got it," Bubba said as he moved toward Russ and helped him out of the trap.

"Jose' this is fantastic! So glad you added this," Russ said as he balanced himself on Jose's shoulder and knocked the sand from the bottom of his shoes.

"Damn that looks great," Ben Triplett said, as his golf cart slowed to a stop. "Just in time, too, Russ. Bubba, thanks so much for jumping on this."

"Ben, come here. Hey Jose'," Russ said, motioning for Jose' to join them. "Show Ben what you did on the back of the green. Jose' proudly led them down the small hill to the back, pointing out the retaining wall first.

"You put a sand trap back here. Aw man, this is sweet! I wish I had my clubs with me."

Jose' asked again for the sand wedge and a ball to be thrown to them. Going through all the similar routine that Russ did, Ben struck the ball. It hit the top of the retaining wall and rolled back toward him just beyond his feet. He set up again and tried a second time. That shot produced the same results.

"Wouldn't be golf if we hit every shot perfectly, would it?" Russ asked Ben.

"The members are going to love this," Ben said excitedly, happy with the addition. "The wall looks great, too. Y'all did a great job. Do you have an invoice for me?"

"This one is on us Ben. Bubba and I talked it over, and we should have built a retaining wall all those years ago. You can't imagine the trouble it would have saved us all," Russ said, glancing at Bubba.

"Wow, wasn't expecting that. Thank you! That will make the board happy."

The crew and Ben Triplett left Russ and Bubba standing at the green. They removed the caution tape and opened the hole for play again. Russ stood with the tape in his hand quietly staring at the green.

"You okay, bud," Bubba asked him, only imagining what he must be thinking.

"You know, I always knew where he was. My secret was safe. His being here meant Mom and I were safe. Right now, I don't feel so safe."

"Well, let's go work on making you feel that way again," Bubba said, as he and Russ both ducked, hearing a loud "Fore!"

They looked toward the source of the disembodied voice and saw a young kid, rounding a tree toward them.

"Sorry."

"Good shot."

"Thanks," the kid said, as he pulled a lob wedge from his bag. He struck the ball, landing it inches from the flag.

"That reminds me of a kid I knew once," Bubba said as he and Russ turned the cart toward the club house.

Russ and Bubba barely made it into the nineteenth hole before Ray Ray ran to them both and gave them a big hug.

"I heard y'all was out here. Y'all want some burgers?"

"Man, yeah that would be great," Bubba responded.

Russ and Bubba sat near the front toward the door.

"I love this place, but it always brings back so many hard memories," Russ said as he stared out onto the area where his father embarrassed him and abused Jaimey so badly the night he killed him.

"Well, just remember the good times. That's all I can tell you," Bubba said as he patted Russ's arm, feeling for his friend.

Russ and Bubba were halfway through their burgers when they saw Jaimey and Nickie pull into the parking lot, and quickly jump out of the car, making their way inside.

"What's going on?"

Taking a big breath, Nickie finally said, "I know where Turtle is."

"What, how?" Russ asked excitedly.

"Long story. I'll tell you on the way. He's in a Hampton Inn in Southaven."

Russ and Bubba jumped up, threw a fifty on the table, and headed north with Nickie in the truck.

CHAPTER FORTY

Paul "Turtle" McCowan sat up in bed and reached for a cigarette. He swung his feet off the side of the bed and rested them on the floor. He noticed he was nude and socks were tied to his wrists. He vaguely remembered something about socks and the red-haired woman.

As she filled his memory, he smiled.

"We must have had one hell of a night," Turtle said softly to himself, as he rubbed his eyes and yawned for several seconds.

He sat quietly in the dark, trying to remember. Trying to remember the sex, but nothing came to him.

"What the hell was her name?" he asked himself, now thinking hard. "P, Pam, Pamela, Presley, Pearl... God, no." Turtle winced at the sound of his mother's name.

He continued thinking, saying out loud every girl's name that started with a P he could think of. He laid back down, still drowsy, and took a long drag from a cigarette. An ember fell on his chest and singed the hair where it fell.

"Shit!" he screamed as he sat up instantly, brushing the ashes from his chest.

He stood and walked into the bathroom, still trying to clear his mind and remember her name.

"Paula, no, dammit," he said as he stood in front of the commode, finished, but unwilling to expend the energy to move. He still felt groggy. He didn't remember the last time he slept so well.

He finally gained strength and walked back toward his cigarettes, extracting another, and reached for his lighter.

"Penny!" he almost shouted to himself as he stared at a shiny copper coin that sat in the middle of his change. He sat staring at the penny. Her hair was almost the same color, and he became excited, horny at the thought of what they must have done.

"I've got to stop drinking so much, I just can't remember," he said out loud to an empty room.

The last thing he remembered was Penny in her panties straddling him, pouring wine down her breasts, letting it trickle into his mouth, and he smiled.

"Damn, how did I get so lucky?" he said out loud again rubbing the corners of his eyes as the smoke irritated them.

He rose and walked to the window, still nude, and opened the blind. The black night stared back at him. The parking lot was empty and still. He glanced at the clock beside his bed. Three thirty. He scratched his crotch and walked away from the window, leaving the blind open. He walked back to his ash tray and snubbed out his cigarette. He lit another one and walked over to the television and turned it on. He flipped through the channels until he came to a movie.

He set the remote back where it originally rested and noticed an unfolded a piece of paper. Small amounts of white powder almost in a perfect half-circle remained on the table.

Damn, we really partied hard tonight. He moistened his middle finger and swiped it over a portion of the white ring and brought it to his mouth.

That don't taste like coke.

He looked again at the ring. He looked toward the bedside table at the two glasses. One full of wine, the other empty. He immediately grabbed the empty one and gingerly sat it within the white circle. It was a perfect fit.

Two college-aged girls walked by the window and stared and pointed at his nude body. He stared back at them. As he moved toward the window, they ran off.

He closed the blinds and stood at the end of the two beds in the room.

I could have sworn when she tied me to the bed it was the bed on the right, but I woke up on the bed on the left.

Turtle looked around the room, his clothes were on the floor in the closet. A few of the drawers in the chest of drawers were partially sticking out.

"Oh, shit no!" he shouted out loud.

He immediately moved to the bed on the right and scooped his hands under the mattress, throwing it off, and exposing an empty void where the duffle bags and suitcase were. Rage filled his mind as he turned his attention to the other bed. He threw the mattress off. Nothing.

"Fuck!" he shouted as loud as he could, pounding his fist into the sheetrock wall, creating a trail of holes.

As if he suddenly remembered something, he moved to his pants that lay in a heap on the floor and rammed his hand into the pockets. All empty. No money, no keys, nothing.

He slipped them on and made his way outside, running

all over the parking lot, searching for his Corvette. He fell to his knees defeated. Everything he had was gone. The money he took from Hugh Jack, the money he stole from Peat, the money he got from his daddy's settlement, his car, all gone.

He slowly walked back into his room. He shut the door and uncorked the remaining bottle of wine, turned it up, and drank the entire contents. He sat on his bed waiting for it to take effect. He just wanted to go back to sleep and never wake up. The room was his until Tuesday. He could at least sleep until then.

Hours later, Turtle woke to a Mexican woman screaming at him and pointing toward the door. She walked all over the room picking up his things and throwing them in a pile. She continued pointing toward the door.

"Time to go," she said.

"No, I'm here until Tuesday; check out is Tuesday."

"Yes! Tuesday," She repeated, pointing toward the ground. "Today Tuesday, you go."

Turtle moved toward the television. He turned it on and flipped through the channels until he came to the news. In the upper right-hand corner of the screen the date and time confirmed what the maid said. It was Tuesday. He had lost two whole days.

He slipped on a t-shirt and started packing his clothes into the small bag he brought with him. He retrieved his toothbrush, comb, and shampoo from the bathroom, threw them into the bag, and started searching for his new Ostrich skin boots.

"Shit!" he screamed. "The bitch took my boots, too."

The Mexican woman became more incensed as he would not move. She pointed to the holes in the wall.

"Those were already there," he said loudly, as if that would help her understand English.

She continued pointing toward the door, pushing him out.

Turtle stood on the black asphalt of the parking lot holding an opened bag with clothes spilling out, barefooted. He took off his t-shirt to fend off the heat and started walking.

He walked down the road that intersected Highway 55 and eventually took a left heading South on 55. He walked in the grass to keep his feet from burning. Every time he saw a Corvette pass, he thought it was his and stared hard at the driver.

This had to be a Guinness Book of World record for the longest walk of shame in history. He thought to himself.

He felt in his pockets to see if he had any change. He had just enough to call and get a ride. He couldn't call Peat as he usually would have. When he thought about him, he simultaneously thought about simply walking into traffic and ending it all right there on Highway 55.

Turtle put the events of three nights ago on rewind. He continued playing it over and over in his head. He couldn't understand how two nights in a row he was taken advantage of by a woman and had his entire world stolen from him. He kept thinking about Penny and how beautiful she was.

I bet we didn't do it.

Bubba, Russ, and Nickie sped up Highway 55 heading north when Nickie spotted a man walking toward them with no shirt on. As the man neared, she saw herself walking down a lonely road, isolated from the world with all of her worldly possessions in a small bag strapped across her back.

As he drew closer, she noticed he wasn't wearing shoes, and as they passed him, she stared into his face.

"That's him, turn around, that's him."

"That's who," Bubba asked.

"Turtle! That's the guy that took me and Hugh Jack into the woods. That's him walkin'. Holy shit!"

Bubba slowed, cut across the median, and headed south. As they passed him on the other side of the interstate, they all strained to see his face.

"I'll be damned. That is Turtle McCowan," Russ almost shouted. "Why in the hell is he walkin'? Where in the hell are his bags? Where in the hell is the suitcase? ... Dammit!"

The anticipation increased with the speed of his truck. Bubba stepped on the gas and came up on Turtle faster than he thought after cresting a small hill. He pulled over and kicked up dust and rocks as he slid to a stop in front of him.

They all jumped out of the truck at one time. Turtle was too defeated to run, and shocked to see Nickie. He remembered her from the day they kidnapped her and Hugh Jack. He stood still, but wide-eyed, as they all approached him.

"You're that girl," Turtle said.

"Yeah, I sure am, you piece of shit. Your dumbass stutterin' brother tried to rape me that day."

"Where's the suitcase?" Russ asked, interrupting Nickie.

"What suitcase?"

"The one with the bones in it. They're mine," Russ said.

"They're gone, along with all my money."

"You mean Hugh Jack's money," Nickie interjected quickly.

"That money was my Daddy's money, and from what I'm hearing, there's more of it somewhere. Hugh Jack stole it, and I'm getting it back from him somehow." Turtle knew his words were empty. He had no plan, no vehicle, no money, no partner, no nothing. Revenge was the last thing he could grasp onto.

"Hugh Jack's dead, you dumbass," Nickie said matter-of-factly.

"What, when?"

"Since his crazy-ass wife shot him right in front of me."

Hearing this news, Turtle felt even more desperate. Every hope to have money, short of having to work for it, was lost. In a split second, he turned and walked into traffic, numb. Cars hit brakes and fishtailed all around him. Smoke from screeching tires filled the road, obscuring the view of other cars behind them. Cars piled into the back of cars. The sound of collapsing metal reverberated all around them. Bubba grabbed Nickie and moved her to safety. Russ raced into the traffic, and pulled Turtle back to the side of the road, and quickly threw him into the back of the truck.

Cars continued rear-ending other cars. A semi-truck began sliding sideways, sending the van portion into the clump of wrecked cars piling up like a cow patty, steaming from the rubber sliding against the asphalt.

Bubba sped along the shoulder of the road and took the first exit, escaping the wreckage as well as the Highway Patrol and drove down a desolate stretch of country road.

CHAPTER FORTY-ONE

The maroon Suburban crested the last hill that led to Bubba Stewart's house. Red O'Halloran sat in the passenger seat as Charlie drove. They parked on the side of the road, turned off the truck, and waited.

Red and Charlie slinked down into their seats as Bubba's girlfriend drove by. She noticed the Suburban on the mainly isolated county road but thought nothing of it since hunting season was just around the corner. However, the maroon Suburban did stick out since pickup trucks were usually seen parked along country roads.

Red slowly passed by Bubba's house. He and Charlie both craning their necks, looking for Bubba's truck. A quick glimpse of a truck speeding away didn't give them much to go on, but Bubba's truck was fitted with specific tool boxes that held the expensive tools of his trade...transit levels, elevation rods, and lasers that sat atop tripods. It was very distinct, used by men who built highways and subdivisions and golf courses. In a small town like Lewiston, his truck stuck out.

Satisfied that the house was empty, they turned down

the driveway. Once inside, they began hurriedly looking. They opened closets emptying the contents. They pulled out drawers, dumping them on the floor. They looked in each of the rooms, searching the only spaces that Red imagined to be large enough to hold several bags of money. Nothing.

Once outside, Red and Charlie immediately went into both storage rooms, turning them upside down, but finding nothing. They finally found the truck in a small barn, but nothing was inside. They had come up empty.

After leaving Bubba's house, Red forced his way into the back door of Capstick Design House with a crowbar.

He and Charlie walked first into a storage room finding nothing. They quickly and quietly started down the long hallway, and were met by "Sticks" Patterson, an employee of Russ's that came to work at Capstick when he followed Russ away from the tour. Stick's face turned red with blood, after Red struck him with the crowbar, knocking him out.

They made their way through the rest of the office. They pilfered each one, turning over desks, pulling out drawers. One by one they made their way through the building until they came to the large conference room attached to Russ's office. They pulled out each drawer of his desk, turned over filing cabinets, and went through the contents of each, making sure they left no stone unturned. Red walked around the large conference room table, staring at the stacks of plans and notes left by Russ and Bubba. At the end of the table were two manila folders. He opened them and poured over the photos of the skeleton, the driver's license, and the ring.

"This is from Hugh," Red excitedly said. "These are the bones we replaced."

Red flipped the manila folder over and found three

sticky notes scribbled in hurried handwriting. Southaven, The South Shall Rise Again bar and social club, the Whispering Pines Motel. Turtle was written and circled several times.

"I think I know where they are, let's go."

CHAPTER FORTY-TWO

Dusk introduced a low-hanging fog that held thick over the pasture behind The South Shall Rise Again bar and social club. The cows that occupied the field were moving toward their place of slumber for the night. Low guttural moans from the field matched the sound coming from the occupied shacks that stood in a row behind the social club.

The cows all stood facing the direction of the shacks, as a door opened revealing a small yellow light inside.

A tall woman with brilliant red hair stumbled to the bottom of the three steps that led from the door and pulled her leather skirt down and smoothed it. She ran her hands inside her bra, pulling and straightening and balancing. She bent down, zipped her boots, and mussed her hair to create volume to the flattened portion in the back. Swinging her bag over her shoulder, she walked in the back door of the social club.

She was followed by Rex, who peered from behind the door of number twelve shack making sure he wasn't seen by anyone, especially the blue-eyed love of his life.

He stood around for a minute and lit a cigarillo. The cheap, pungent smell filled the air. The occasional growing glow from the tip was the only indication he was there, as he stood motionless in the black cloudy night. A thick fog rolled toward him, and before long, the small ember from the cigarillo was obscured and almost invisible.

He used the fog, walking through it to make his way unseen toward the front of the building. As he neared the front corner, he stood for a long time watching as the slow weeknight customers meandered through the parking lot toward the front door.

The burn from his cigarillo turned bright orange as he sucked in, alerting his presence to the eyes of a few regulars. They quietly waved. He hoped they would just leave him alone.

He adjusted his stance, leaned his shoulder on the corner of the building where he stood, and stared at the half-smoked stick between his fingers. He thought about going home, but couldn't run out on the poker game that started in an hour. He watched as the genesis of a small skirmish began to form. He let out a sharp loud whistle between his fingers that quickly replaced the cigarillo. The two grown men at the door moved quickly to the men who had yet to make it inside and turned them back toward their cars.

With a nod of their heads, they acknowledged his presence, as they walked back to their posts. The crunch of gravel under moving tires sounded as a new car crept into the parking lot, searching for a parking place.

Rex stubbed the cigarillo on the side of his building. He threw the butt down and screwed the silver tip of his boots into the smoldering tobacco, before he bent down to pick it up.

He walked through the front door and was immediately met by the blue-eyed woman.

"Where have you been, sugar? I've been looking all over for you." She draped her arms around his shoulders and locked her fingers behind his neck. She raised herself to kiss him gently on the lips, but recoiled and screwed up her face in disgust. "Those damn cigars," she said as she wiped her mouth and made her way to the bar for a drink to filter the taste.

Penny walked by with a tray of beers floating in the air and winked at Rex. A slight grin came across his lips. He watched her walk by, and as he turned around, he stared directly into the blue eyes of the one who just had her arms wrapped around him. He ignored her. She hated seeing the two of them together.

Rex's office was a smaller reflection of the rest of the social club. Two pool tables and three poker tables took up most of the floor space. To the side of his desk was a six-foot "mini bar" stocked with pre-orders from the participants of "poker night."

Three blonde women with skinny waists, large breasts, and big hair, wearing wifebeaters and skinny shorts that didn't cover much, floated around the room preparing the tables. Chip trays were placed in the center of each. Two tackle boxes full of every denomination of cash were set at each table along with a carousel of poker chips.

Rex sat at his desk going over the seating chart, pairing the regulars and the newer players. He motioned for an associate as he heard the familiar knock at the back door.

Sheriff Guillroy Tate took his cowboy hat off as he walked through the back door. Rex motioned for everyone to leave as he stood and greeted the sheriff, handing him a small manila envelope.

"I've got some heavy hitters coming in tonight. I'm going to need your boys to leave them alone."

"No problem," the sheriff said as he crammed the envelope in his back pocket.

"I need you to check on something for me," Rex said as he made his way behind his desk.

He bent over, and picked up the leather suitcase, plopped it on his desk and opened it. He twirled the suitcase around, revealing the contents inside.

"Holy hell! Where in the hell did that come from?"

"You don't need to worry about that right now," Rex said as he reached into the skinny side pocket on the suitcase and extracted Randy's driver's license. "I need you to run this and tell me what you can find out about him."

"Okay, no problem. Looks like he's been gone a while."

"It does appear so."

The sheriff left through the same back door he came in. As he did, Rex let out a piercing whistle and the hostesses followed by the poker players made their way through the door.

CHAPTER FORTY-THREE

Bubba, Russ, Nickie, and Turtle made it to the Whispering Pines Motel just across the Tennessee line.

"Man, what the hell was that all about back there? You just about got the two of us killed. And by the way, I'm not calling you Turtle any more. I'm calling you Paul. That's a stupid nickname," Russ said.

Paul sat quiet and motionless. His eyes were fixed, staring straight ahead, not blinking.

"I wish you had just let me be. I got nothing left. They took my money ..."

"Hugh Jack's money," Nickie quickly interjected again.

"My daddy's money," Paul corrected her as he gave Nickie an icy stare. "They took my new 'vette," Paul finished his sentence and bent over planting his face in his hands, softly crying.

"And they took my bon... ah, suitcase," said Russ. "We have to get that back. Do you know who took it?" Russ asked, almost not wanting to hear the answer, for fear he would have no clue where it was.

"No, well I do, but I don't," Paul said slowly, barely, continuing to stare at the same spot on the wall that he found and became fixated on moments earlier. "I don't have anything left, nothing."

"Look at me dumbass. If you will help us, I will give you the money you lost. How much was it?"

Paul turned and looked at Nickie. His countenance immediately improved.

"I'm not sure. I had the fifty-thousand from my daddy's settlement and the rest was the money I got from Hugh Jack. I never counted it. You don't look like you have any money."

"Okay, well look. If you'll help Russ get that suitcase back, I'll be sure you at least get your money back and possibly your corvette too, deal?"

"Yeah, okay."

Paul's interest immediately improved.

"By the way, where's that bitch brother of yours that tried to rape me?"

"Oh Peat? He's, he's home ... somewhere."

"We went to your nasty-ass house with all the turtle shells hangin' everywhere, and we didn't see Peat nowhere," Nickie said noticing an odd look on Paul's face.

"Look, can we get back to the suitcase? Tell us what happened," Russ asked, as he and Bubba pulled up a chair and began listening.

"I went to a bar..."

The South Shall Rise Again? Bubba asked.

"Yeah, how'd you know?"

"Your momma told us. We visited with Pearl. She told us you might be up here," Russ answered.

Suddenly Paul's demeanor changed to that of a little boy. The brash, cocky, sure criminal Nickie first met was now nothing more than a scared, defeated little boy. As Paul talked, images of Peat and his mother flipped through his mind.

The look on Peat's face as he stood with the arrow sticking out of his chest was stamped on his memory. He had killed him to keep all the money, and now it was all gone. He killed him for nothing. As it turned out, he had gotten used to Peat's stuttering because he now missed it.

Russ' fingers were snapping in front of Paul's face as he regained consciousness and heard Russ.

"Paul, tell the rest, go ahead, finish."

"I was at The South Shall Rise Again, two nights before. I was jumped and beat pretty good. They stole the money I had in my pockets, two pretty good rolls of cash. I went back the next night to try to find the woman that was with me when I got jumped. I figured she was in on it. She never showed up. The next night I met this good-lookin' red-headed woman with green eyes. She drank with me most of the night. I took her back to my hotel room. We was pretty drunk, or at least I was, not to mention I'm pretty sure she drugged me. I found some white powder on the dresser by the wine bottles where she poured our drinks. I had the bags and that suitcase hid good, under the bed. Don't know how they found them or why they even thought I had money at all."

"Well, I can guess. You show up in a bar with fat rolls of cash, driving a brand-new Corvette. You should never advertise it. I'm sure you wanted the women to see your big rolls of cash. I'm sure you were probably talking about your recent windfall trying to impress," Russ said, more than a little disgusted.

Paul quietly nodded, shrinking more and more into the shell of a little boy.

"During the night, did this lady say where she was from?"

"No not at all, nothing. I feel sure she probably works for Rex, the owner. That bar I hear is a front for all kinds of illegal goins on. They got shacks in the back for hookers to work in, illegal poker games, gun runnin'. I seen the sheriff come in there a few times but he never done nothin'."

"Would you know that woman if you saw her again?" Bubba asked.

"Oh, hell yeah, I would. I'm in love with her."

Russ rolled his eyes and slowly shook his head.

"If she sees him coming, she'll know he knows what she did. We just need a good description."

"Huny and Bandit seen her," Paul said to no one in particular.

"Who did you say," Nickie asked, confused. "Did you say Huny and Bandit?"

"Yeah, they're friends of mine, they sell a little dope for me, here and there. They was there that night helpin' me to try and catch the woman from the first night. They saw the red- headed woman. They go to the social club all the time. Do you know them?"

"Yeah, I do actually," Nickie said with a confused grin.

"We've got to have a plan. We can't just waltz up in there and ask for the suitcase, full of old bones, back," Russ said, as he let out a long, frustrated breath.

"Do you think this woman would help us if we could find her?"

"If you have money. That usually does a lot to convince people. I think she would be all about the money."

"I've got an idea. You say you know this Bandit and what is the other name?"

"Huny," Nickie said, remembering how she spelled it for her the day they met.

"They are always at the store on the way to golf course."

"Fants Grocery. Where the old gas station was on the right side of the road across from that old factory?" Russ asked.

"I guess," Nickie said.

"Let's get Jaimey on the phone, get her to go find them and get them on the phone with you," Russ said to Nickie. "Okay if she gets a few rolls of cash to bring with her?"

"Of course," Nickie said.

The phone woke Jim and Jaimey. They had fallen asleep on the couch after Jim got home from the office. A groggy hello was met with an excited Russ on the other end.

"Jim, let me talk to Mom please."

"Who is it," Jaimey asked with her eyes still closed, yawning.

"Russ," he said as he handed the receiver to her.

"Hey, babe."

"Mom, listen, we think we know where they are, but I've got to get a few things from home."

"Okay, what?"

"Listen carefully. First thing in the morning I need you to go to Fants Grocery. Hopefully there will be an older couple there whose names are Bandit and Huny. When you see them, take them to the pay phone and call this number. I'm going to need them to bring me a few things. I need you to get a few rolls of cash from one of the bags in the room off the garage and give it to them. I need them to get on the way tomorrow, so I will need to speak to them first thing in the morning. Okay?"

"Got it. Russ ... be careful."

"Yes, ma'am."

"And tell Bubba and Nickie to be careful, too. How is she?"

"Still feisty. We're fine."

Night

The fight didn't take long. Russ was exhausted from the day. His eyes closed with the darkness and from the darkness, eyes stared back at him. Sets of eyes speckled through the woods, blinking, opening, then closing in perfect rhythm. They continued staring, as Russ took them in, fighting against the fear they created, trying to steady his heart. He opened and closed his own eyes hoping they would dissipate with his own blindness, but when he opened them, they remained unmoved. The quiet woods surrounding them began to wake. Frogs and crickets started a deafening rhythm, singing to each other. The eyes soon converged into one and sunk into the earth. The ground before him moved, shuttered. A singular burrowed mound finally reached him, coming up through the ground standing before him. Dirt and flesh finally covered the bones that had only shown themselves bare. The fleshed-out image appeared before him sneering, angry.

"You've lost me again; you never could do anything right." His father's face was as dirty as the last time he saw him alive. He was dressed the same, he displayed the same sneer on his face. His scent permeated Russ's memory. Mainly sweat, cow manure, beer, and body odor. His face appeared in and out of the dark, appearing and disappearing as if he were in a rocking chair, rocking in and out of the light. Almost as if he couldn't make up his mind, to stay or go. And then as the light disappeared, he did as well, pulled back again into the dark earth. He woke to a ringing.

CHAPTER FORTY-FOUR

Russ and Bubba woke together and reached for the phone at the same time, their hands fighting each other's. Bubba finally lifted it from its receiver and held it to his ear.

"I was told to call this here number, for a ... Russ?"

Bubba handed the phone to Russ.

"Hello," he said groggily into the phone.

"Yeah, they's this woman here, told me to call this number."

"Yeah, yeah, is this, om ... Bandit?"

"That's me. Huny's here, too," Bandit said, smiling into the phone.

"Hold on just a minute, please," Russ said as he began beating on the adjoining door.

"Nickie, Nickie. Bandit's on the phone. Nickie."

Soon the door opened, and Nickie stood in front of Russ in only her bra and panties trying to wake up.

"Bandit, hey this is Nickie."

"How are you, young'un?"

"I'm fine. Look, can you and Huny make another trip to Southaven today? We need your help."

"Aw, I don't know. Me and Huny's got a singin' tonight down south."

"Bandit I need you. I need you to cancel that and do me this favor today. I'll pay you."

"Yeah, this lady's trying to give me rolls of cash right now. I don't know her. I ain't wantin' to get in trouble."

"That's my money, Bandit. I told her to give it to you. Some of it I'll need when you get here, but the other part of it is yours."

"Hold on."

Nickie could hear Bandit as he turned to Huny and repeated what she had just told him.

"Some of all that money is ours?" she could hear Huny asking Bandit.

"That's what she said."

There was a long silence.

"Okay, we'll do it."

"Great! I'm putting you back on the phone with Russ, okay?"

"Bandit, thank you so much for doing this. I need you to take the money from my mom and bring it to me. I also need you to bring me one other thing."

"Okay, what's that?"

"Do you know the old grocery warehouse across from the old Ford place?"

"Yeah. Sure do."

"I need you to go around to the side door and let yourself in. Once you're in there, you should see a leather suitcase on the floor. I need you to bring that with you. And Bandit, I need you here as soon as you can get here. We're staying at the Whispering Pines Motel in Southaven."

"I know that place. Me and Huny's been there before."

"Okay great. See you soon."

Bubba walked over to Paul who was still asleep on the floor and softly kicked him to wake him.

"Get out of the way. I've got to use the bathroom," Bubba said as he continued nudging Paul.

Bubba was unable to hide his dislike of Paul McCowan. His sixth sense about people sounded alarms when he was around Paul. Paul gave off vibes of dishonesty and laziness. He had a criminal feeling to him that Bubba noticed. There was something else too. More than what he already knew about the stolen money and the torture of Hugh Jack and Nickie. He could tell he was holding on to something.

He always felt that Russ had done the same thing, held on to something, too, but could never put his finger on it. He thought Russ might have just acted aloof and distant at times because of his childhood, but then when Russ told him what he did, how he killed Randy, that all went away. A confessed spirit cleanses the soul, does a body good. Paul had something he needed to confess. Bubba felt it. He knew it.

Nickie opened the door to Huny and Bandit standing on the other side holding rolls of cash and the leather suitcase with toothless smiles on their faces. Their palms were opened as if they were making an offering to her.

"What are you doing? Get in here," Nickie said as she grabbed each of them by the wrist and pulled them into the room.

The room grew much smaller with them all crowded inside.

"Hell, Turtle, what are you doin' here?" Huny asked, smiling, almost shouting.

"Hey, keep your voices down. These walls are thin," Russ said, excitedly.

"That red-headed woman, Penny, stole some stuff from me, out of my room. That suitcase belongs to Russ here. We need to help him get it back. She took my 'vette."

"Well how did you get all that?" Bandit asked, no longer smiling.

"Hugh Jack had possession of it, and I stole some things from Hugh Jack. It was with the bags I stole from him. Now Penny has stolen that from me. It's very important. We need to get it back, and we need y'all's help."

"Well, what can we do?"

They all took seats on the beds and chairs available, and Russ mapped out the plan.

"They will be watching for Paul to come back into the bar to find Penny, so he can't just show up again. That will ruin our chances of talking with Penny."

"Who's Paul?" Bandit asked, wearing a confused face.

"Turtle," Nickie chimed in. "Turtle is Paul's nickname."

"Oh, well I'll be, I didn't know." Bandit said, thoughtfully.

"Bandit they are used to you being in there. You know what she looks like, so I just need you to point her out to me," Russ said.

"Oh, you ain't gon' miss her, she's the only redhead in the place. Built like a brick house on stilts. She's fine as hell," Bandit said as Huny lightly punched him.

"Jealous?" Bandit asked, smiling at Huny.

Russ laid out his plan for the group. Everyone knew their role.

Huny listened closely to the detailed, somewhat complex plan, and raised her hand. "What do you want me to do?"

"Whatever you normally do." Russ said, and this satisfied Huny. A look of relief washing over her face.

"What about my money and my car? Are we gonna get that back?" Turtle asked again.

"If I see it, and it's easy pickins, I'll grab it, too."

"I done told you I would give you the money you lost," Nickie said to Turtle, clearly irritated.

"Well, what about my car and ...,"

"You keep on and you're not getting shit back," Nickie said, staring Turtle down until his eyes shifted toward the floor.

Turtle started diving down a deep hole again. He couldn't just let it go. His money and car were stolen from him. It stuck in his craw. Anger kept building. In his mind he had finally gotten on top and then, as always, it was taken from him. Taken because of his ignorance, because of his weakness for women. The one thing that always got in the way... women.

CHAPTER FORTY-FIVE

Penny sat in the middle of the bed and slid her feet into her stilettos, smoothing her leather pants as she did. The row of shacks were numbered one through twelve. Number twelve belonged to her and Rex. The other girls knew to stay away and so far, as far as they knew, Rex's girlfriend knew nothing about the two of them and their time in number twelve.

Three light taps rattled the door. Penny and Rex locked eyes. Soon two more light taps confirmed that the person on the other side of the door was one of Rex's men.

Penny opened the door and waved the man inside.

"Rex, Guillroy's here. Said he needs to talk to you."

"Where's is she?"

"She ain't here. Coast is clear."

The three of them walked the twenty yards across the wide road between the social club and the shacks, and slipped into the backdoor of Rex's office.

"Sheriff Tate, how are you," Rex asked as he poured the sheriff a bourbon and handed it to him.

"I got some information for you."

Sheriff Tate turned his glass up and finished the whisky in one loud gulp.

"Randy Crawford was reported missing by his wife back in the eighties. He was in his late thirties. One child, a son named Russ. No other children. At one time, he had a very successful real estate development company and lost everything when the casinos came into the coast. They lived in Biloxi, moved to Lewiston. No other living relatives. The wife reported at the time that he had a bad drinking problem. They finally chalked it up to a drunken accident, figured he was lyin' in a ditch somewhere and would eventually turn up. Never did."

"Why in the hell is he laying in that suitcase in my office?" Rex asked as he pointed toward the case holding Randy's remains. "The fact that his remains are in that suitcase tells me that he was probably murdered. What do you think, Sheriff?"

"I think you're right. I need to find that fella that last had these. Penny said they were at the Hampton Inn in Southaven. Name was Paul, nickname was ..."

"Turtle," Penny answered.

"That's all I have. I would imagine that he or whoever put these remains in this suitcase will be here pretty soon. See what you can find out at the hotel and let me know, hear."

The sheriff stood, lingering.

"Oh, forgive me, Gil. Your campaign contribution." Rex opened a small safe behind him and took out a thousand dollars and handed it to the sheriff.

"Thank you, Gil."

CHAPTER FORTY-SIX

The silence of the cool autumn day was interrupted by the crackle of a walkie talkie.

Bandit walked out the front door of The South Shall Rise Again bar excitedly and loudly whispered into a walkie talkie.

"Redhead walking out behind me. That's her. That's Penny."

Penny walked out of the front door of the social club several seconds behind Bandit. She stopped just outside the door and applied lipstick and then pushed one corner of her sunglasses more snugly on her nose. She was draped in jewelry. Bangle bracelets dangled from her wrist. Her purse strap lay in her bent elbow. A large, rust-colored beaded necklace attracted even more attention to her low-cut neck line. Her legs were long and athletic and covered in leather pants that held tight to her skin. She looked ready to shoot a video for MTV. She walked with confidence and purpose as she extracted car keys from her purse and unlocked the door to the Corvette.

"There's my damn car," Turtle said as he reached for the door. " She's getting in my damn 'vette."

Bubba leaned over, stopping him from getting out of the car, and jerked his body back toward his.

"Dammit, Paul. I told you, just be cool, and we'll get your damn car back," Russ said, now sorry he made the decision to bring him along.

She pulled the Corvette out onto the paved road, burning the back tires as she did. A curtain of white smoke blanketed the road as the rear fishtailed, finally straightening out.

"Dammit, she's burnin' all my rubber off," Turtle said, almost crying in the back seat.

"If she's going to go this fast, this might be tough keeping up with her, especially without letting on that we're following her," Russ said.

"You've got to keep up with her," Paul cried from the back seat. "It's all I have."

The walkie talkie crackled again. Bandit and Huny brought up the rear of the convoy.

"I heard her tell she was goin' to get her nails painted," Bandit said, almost screaming.

The county roads soon ended, and traffic began to thicken. As she approached the outskirts of town, they caught up with her and were able to follow her more closely, making sure to keep a safe distance between them.

She meandered through traffic and cut through a residential neighborhood that eventually flowed into a small strip mall. She shot across the road and parked in the center of the parking lot.

Russ pulled up right behind her, and they all watched as her long legs that ended in stiletto heels poured out of the door like honey. Her long body unfolded from the Corvette and she locked it.

"Paul, don't feel bad. Now I see how she was able to take advantage of you. I would have fallen for her, too," Bubba said, mesmerized by her form.

She was elegant, too sophisticated for The South Shall Rise Again bar and social club, and Russ wondered why she was there.

Penny walked into a nail salon. Russ had Bandit pull his van into the parking space beside the Corvette. They swapped vehicles with Bandit and Huny and waited.

"What makes a woman, good lookin' and sophisticated as she is, work in a place like that social club?" Russ asked no one in particular.

"Money," Paul said. "They's a lot of it in that place. She's a good-lookin' hooker, that's all she is. Don't let her looks fool you. She's a redneck just like me. Just a little smarter's all."

"I've got to pee," Nickie said as she squirmed in her seat. "I ain't gon' be able to hold it."

As soon as Russ was about to say run in and we'll wait for you, Penny exited the nail solon and turned right. She walked down past several stores and finally made her way into "The Tat Cat" tattoo shop.

"Go ahead, Nickie. This could take a while," Russ said, as he laid his seat back and closed his eyes.

"I've got to go, too."

"You're not going anywhere, here use this," Russ said, handing an empty Gatorade container to Paul.

"In here?"

"I'm sure it's not the first time you've peed in a car," Bubba said.

Soon the back seat sounded like rain falling on a plastic bucket.

"Oh, crap that was quick, there she is."

"I can't cut it off," Paul said from the back seat. "Oh shit."

Paul got nervous and wet himself trying to stop the flow. As Penny headed toward the car, Nickie exited at the same time, and they walked beside each other. Nickie locked eyes with Russ. The reality of the situation made her stomach turn.

Russ moved into the passenger side of the middle bench seat as Bubba exited the driver's side of the van. As Penny stood at her door opening it, Bubba grabbed her and forced her quickly into the open door behind her.

Penny fought with everything she had. Her long legs kicked and flailed as her hands bore down on Bubba's back as hard as she could hit him. Cussing, she spit on Bubba before she looked into the back seat, shocked to see Paul as he zipped his pants.

She knew she had been caught when she saw Paul's face, as shocked as it was, and she slowly calmed herself. She quickly realized she sat sandwiched between Russ and Bubba.

"You might as well calm down. You're not going anywhere," Russ said. "We just need your help."

Paul grabbed her from behind around her neck, "Give me my damn car back, bitch."

She began kicking and fighting again. Nickie quickly turned to watch the commotion. She moved her nimble body, and brought her small foot up and kicked Penny in the stomach as she began fighting Bubba again, trying to exit the van.

"Calm down, dammit!"

"Look, everybody just calm down. We just want to talk to you," Russ said with his hands held up in surrender, trying to calm the situation.

"First of all, …" Russ started but was interrupted by Paul.

"No, first of all, give me my damn car keys," Paul shouted, letting out the built-up frustration he had carried for the last few days.

"Where's my damn money, too?"

"The money is gone."

"Where?" Russ chimed in.

"You won't get it back. It's gone."

"I'm not worried about the money. Where is the suitcase?"

"You mean with the dead body in it? Rex thought someone would show up looking for that," Penny said as she looked down at a broken nail.

"I just had these done, you asshole!"

"I need your help," Russ said, as he held up a large wad of money with a thick rubber band around it.

"I don't know what you want me to do, but whatever it is, it'll take a lot more than that."

Russ stared at Nickie, and she nodded her approval.

"Help me and you got it."

"It'll take four of those rolls," Penny said.

"Done."

"Five since it was that easy."

"Done. I've got to have those bones back. The money will pay for your help, and an extra roll will pay for your silence, so six rolls."

Penny adjusted herself in the seat, and everyone calmed down a bit. Her labored breathing slowed, and she looked again at her nails.

Paul grabbed a wash rag from the floor of the van and dried himself.

"Let me outta here so I can get in my 'vette and go home."

"Wait a minute, Paul. She has to go back in your car so nothing looks out of place. If we show up with her in here, how in the hell will she explain that? You'll get your car back … just be patient."

"I thought your damn name was Turtle or some dumbass shit like that," Penny said, frowning at Paul.

"Turtle's a nickname. Paul's my real name. How many other men have you done this to, anyway?"

"I've lost count. Fifty maybe?"

"Can we get back to the matter at hand please?" Russ asked, frustrated with the small talk.

"I have another suitcase with remains in it …," Russ started until he was interrupted by Penny.

"Damn! What did y'all do? Rob a bunch of graves or something?"

"The bones your boss has are the bones of my father."

"Oh shit, sorry," Penny immediately felt bad for Russ.

"If we could somehow switch them out so he's not alarmed, we'll be on our way. You'll have the money, less a new Corvette," Russ said as he glanced at Paul. "And everybody will have what they want, we'll be on our way, and this will be over. The other remains are in a matching suitcase, so he shouldn't expect anything until it's too late."

"The suitcase is in his office, sitting behind his desk, waiting for you to show up. That office is always full of people though. The good thing is the suitcase is also right by the back door. He keeps that door locked. He is the only one with a key. And then there's his girlfriend. She's always around."

"Who?" Bubba asked.

"Let me guess. Big black hair, short shorts, blue eye liner, and pantyhose," Paul asked.

"That's her. She's Rex's girlfriend. I can get him away from the office, but like I said, it'll be locked, and he is the only one with a key."

"How will you get him away? Where would you take him?" Nickie asked.

"Well, I am Rex's friend with benefits let's say. The number twelve shack behind the club is ours. It sits directly across from his office door. We usually meet there at the end of the night when everything is closed up. If you can wait, that will be the best time do get the suitcase. Everyone will be gone."

"Shack?" Bubba asked.

"They got some screwin' shacks in the back, twelve of 'em," Paul offered.

"What all goes on in this club?" Russ asked.

"A little bit of everything. Prostitution, gun running. Rex has a huge still out in the woods. He sells moonshine all over the state of Mississippi and parts of Tennessee."

"And of course, don't forget your specialty—seduction and theft," Paul threw in. "What was that you put in my drink the other night anyway?"

"Molly. It's a date rape drug," Penny said, matter-of-factly. "He has a small drug ring also."

"You know I'm in love with you," Paul said, reaching his hand toward her.

"Damn! This just got increasingly more difficult," Russ said, a feeling of fear and dread dissolved his bravado. "I don't think we can just walk in and walk out."

"I'm tellin' you, you need to wait until the end of the night when everybody will be gone. Rex and I will be in the number twelve shack. I can signal you with the light outside the shack. He always takes a shower before we get down to business. When he goes in, I'll get the keys and hand them to you. You can slip in, swap the suitcases, return the key, and he'll never know."

Russ looked at Bubba and Nickie. "Sounds good to me. That just might work."

"Sounds like a plan to me," Bubba said as he drew his shoulders toward his ears and held his palms toward heaven.

"Penny, you drive the Corvette back to the bar and leave the keys in the ignition. Paul, as soon as she's inside and no one is paying attention, you can get back in your car and drive back home. Nickie, ask Bandit and Huny to stay in town in case we need them for anything ... just in case we need to develop a contingency plan. We'll get them a room at the motel."

"And by the way, where's my boots?" Turtle asked still barefoot.

"In the backseat of your 'vette."

Penny stepped out of the van, adjusted her clothes, got back into the Corvette and drove back to the bar. Russ, Bubba, and Turtle followed close behind her. As soon as she got out, disappeared into the bar, and no one was looking, Turtle jumped out and into his car and turned the Corvette South. The rest drove back to the Whispering Pines Motel. They heard phones ringing as they approached the room. Bubba quickly unlocked the door and grabbed the phone.

Jaimey was on the line, frantic.

"Bubba someone has broken into your house and the office. They've trashed them both."

Bubba plopped down on the bed, exhausted.

"Okay, I'm on my way home. Is everybody okay?"

"Yes, just shaken up is all. Sticks was hit over the head, but he'll be okay."

Bubba told Russ and Nickie what Jaimey said.

"Someone's looking for the money. Bubba why don't you get Bandit and Huny to take you home and you deal with that. Nickie and I will handle tonight."

"Are you sure you two will be okay?"

"We'll be fine. Home has to be dealt with, too. Hopefully we will see you tomorrow."

"Okay, be careful," Bubba said as he hugged them both.

CHAPTER FORTY-SEVEN

Sheriff Tate sat at his desk, nursing a fresh toothpick, as he stared out of his window into the blackened sky. He stood, took his gun belt off, loosened his pants, and sat again reclining in his chair. He had finally eaten the lunch special he missed earlier in the day and closed his eyes. He was drifting off to sleep when his secretary's voice broke his quiet solitude.

"Sheriff, Moana from the Whispering Pines Motel is on line one. You want me to take a message since it's so late?"

"No, I'll take it. Thank you."

"This is Guillroy."

"Sheriff, you told me to call you if I saw anything strange goin' on over here."

"Yes, Moana. Whatcha' got?"

"Well, there is about three men staying in one room, number sixteen. There's a young little thing staying in the adjoining room, and earlier they got another room for this couple. The man's name is Bandit, of all things. It just looks odd to me."

"Okay, does one of the men fit the description I gave

you? Is one named Russ?"

"They paid with cash. The big fella that paid… let me see here … his name was Bubba, not sure about a Russ."

"Okay, thank you, Moana. You said room number sixteen, correct?"

"Yes sir."

Moana hung up the phone, leaned toward the window, and looked out into the parking lot. A maroon Suburban had remained in the same parking spot since dusk. She saw the occasional tiny red glow followed by a small cloud of smoke as it filtered through the crack in the window. She assumed he was a pimp or a husband or boyfriend, waiting. Couples made their way toward their rooms. A man pushing a shopping cart, containing all of his worldly possessions, slowly walked his usual route to the dugouts at the baseball field behind the motel. A man had a young woman by her elbow walking her quickly toward their room.

Moana had watched her small world go by just outside the large picture window of the office for the last thirty years. She graduated from high school on Friday night, and started work there on Saturday morning, and she never left except that one week when she went to Florida.

She watched as the man in the Suburban finally got out and walked toward the row of rooms obscured from her view as Sheriff Tate parked his cruiser in front of her office.

"They were here earlier Gil but left right after it got dark," Moana said.

"Moana, thanks for keeping an eye out," the Sheriff said as he handed her a fifty-dollar bill.

"No problem hun. You come back to see me if Shelly stops takin' care of you now," Moana said, winking as the sheriff walked out of the front door.

CHAPTER FORTY-EIGHT

Red had let himself into the room with a credit card and opened the door only slightly at first, as he slowly crept inside. He quietly walked to the closed bathroom door and quickly thrust it open, his gun entering first.

The room was empty. He looked around and rifled through a few pieces of clothing. Both beds appeared to have been slept in. A pallet was on the floor.

He walked to the nightstand between the beds and saw scrawled on a notepad, The South Shall Rise Again bar and social club. Turn by turn directions were written neatly, and he picked up the pad and tore it off.

He turned toward the door when Sherriff Tate bounded into the room with his gun drawn. Red quickly reached for his, and as he did, Sherriff Tate pumped three rounds in his chest. Red fell against a bed and slowly slid down toward the floor holding his chest. He coughed up white foaming blood, spitting as he coughed. His hand slowly fell to his side, and his eyes never moved again.

Sherriff Tate closed the door and walked to the body. He

rolled him over onto his back and removed his pistol from his waist. He then felt around for a wallet and pulled it from his back pocket. He opened it expecting to see Russ Crawford's Identification.

O'Halloran was the name on the card. He bent down to feel for a pulse, unable to find one, and slowly pushed the man's eyes closed. He felt around in the other pockets and pulled a piece of paper from his hand. Scrawled across the top was The South Shall Rise Again bar and social club. Below that were directions to the bar. It was written on Whispering Pines Hotel stationary. He found loose cash and kept it. He replaced his service revolver in its holster, and pulled out his handkerchief from his back pocket. He wiped down Red's pistol and opened his hand, closing it around the grip.

CHAPTER FORTY-NINE

Russ and Nickie parked along the railroad tracks that ran beside the bar. Clouds rolled slowly across the full moon, turning the night sky an ominous dark, swirling gray, the stars only visible as the clouds parted allowing them to shine bright.

"Looks a little like Van Gogh's 'Starry Night,' doesn't it?" Russ asked out loud.

"Who?" Nickie asked, unsure of who Van Gogh was or for that matter what "Starry Night" was.

City street lights were a luxury that didn't reach this far into the county. The only light at all was a lone bulb burning on each end of the bar's front entrance.

A light fog continued to roll in from the river that flowed behind the club and swept across the lights of the last car leaving.

Russ started the car and slowly crept along the barren stretch of road. He turned into the parking lot and parked at the opposite end near the number one shack, being sure to stay as far from the number twelve shack as possible.

Penny was inside working her magic. Rex was like putty to her, he was never able to turn down her advances.

"Why don't you go take a shower? I'll be right here waiting for you when you get through," Penny said to Rex as she patted the bed beside her.

As soon as she heard the shower turn on, she reached inside his pants and felt for his keys and dropped them. Rex opened the door and saw her standing there with his keys and pants in her hands.

"What are you doing?"

"I was just moving your pants and your keys fell out."

Rex walked back into the bathroom and closed the door. She took the single office key from the ring and replaced the keys in his pocket.

Russ and Nickie sat waiting until they saw the light outside the number twelve shack turn to black. That was their cue. He quickly walked toward the number twelve shack, stood beside the door, and waited until Penny opened the door and gave him the key.

"Hurry. It usually doesn't take him long," she whispered.

Russ and Nickie slipped through the darkness toward the office door. Russ opened the door and handed the key to Nickie. Nickie ran it back across to Penny, and she shut the door behind her.

"Let's get in and out quickly. Penny said they wouldn't be long."

Russ immediately found Randy's remains. The suitcase was right where Penny said it would be. He switched the cases, and placed the one with Randy's remains on Rex's desk and opened it to be sure the remains were inside. He shone the lights in different areas of the suitcase until he finally found the ID that was inside. He stared at his father's photo. The picture was taken in happier times when Randy was sober and had thick, long hair. His face was rounder than he ever remembered, and he wore a slightly crooked smile. A pain grew in the pit of his stomach.

The reflection of light bounced off framed photos tracked along the wall as Nickie stalked the history of the social club.

Russ continued staring at the photo. It transported him to a time he only wished he knew again. He stared at a man he didn't know, and a pang of sorrow flowed over his body in a hot wash. Guilt began to take residence. He couldn't take his eyes off the man, wondering what his life would have been like if the man in the photo had been a real father.

His trance was broken by a shrill cry, followed by the sound of broken glass. He looked up to see Nickie clawing the photos off the wall and slamming them down on the ground. A long deep guttural sound, interrupted by bouts of sobbing, came from Nickie. Her body convulsed violently as she cried.

Russ ran to her, concerned about the noise. He grabbed her and hugged her to him.

"What is it? What's wrong? Shh."

Nickie pointed to the photo on the floor. Russ reached it and turned it over. Through sobs, Nickie wasn't able to speak well. She stuttered as she spoke.

"That's Dddanny... Williams," she said as she pointed a shaking finger toward the picture. The man in the photo was in several others covering the wall.

Russ hugged her tighter.

"He's one of them," Nickie said through continued sobs.

"Who, what?" Russ asked, not understanding.

"The man in the picture," she said pointing to Rex, "I remember him from when I was little, right after I was taken, I was 'rented' to that man for several hours at a time by Danny Williams. He was in and out of Biloxi all the time," Nickie said as she swiped her hand over her face and nose.

She immediately jumped up and ran into the bar. She began throwing whisky and vodka and rum bottles against the wall, breaking them. The bar soon smelled like a working distillery.

Russ saw again the pain she was in as she picked up a wooden baseball bat. She swiped through several bottles at a time behind the bar.

"Come here," Russ said as he led her into the stock room where case upon case of spirits were stacked on top of each other. They both picked up one case after the other and slammed them on the ground. Whiskey poured out all over the floor. They picked up individual bottles and flung them against the brick wall. They backed out of the room as it began to flood, filling their noses and making them grimace.

"Follow me," Russ said, as he handed Nickie a bottle of Jack Daniels.

Nickie threw it against the wall.

"No, no, no, don't throw this one," Russ said as he handed Nickie another one.

"Go stand next to the door and wait for me."

Nickie made it by the door as Russ backed toward her, spilling a full bottle onto the ground. He grabbed the curtain on the window behind Rex's desk and tore it.

"Get the suitcase and go take it to the car, quickly."

Nickie delivered the suitcase and made it back to the office door. Russ was shoving a strip of the curtain into the mouth of the Jack Daniels bottle and lit it with a lighter from Rex's desk.

"Okay, throw it right in the middle of the room."

She did, and as it hit the floor it burst into spreading flames. The fire caught on in seconds and immediately jumped up and spread into the stock room. Within seconds the stock room was fully engulfed in flames. Russ and Nickie ran back to the car and waited for Penny.

Before they reached the car, Rex ran out of the number twelve shack pulling on his pants as he ran into his office. He soon reappeared throwing VHS tapes and a duffle bag out the door. He made a second trip and another pile of tapes were thrown to the ground. Penny ran toward the car in her bra and panties, holding her dress and shoes, a look of terror frozen on her face.

"What in the hell happened? What happened to a quiet in and out?" she screamed.

"Your boss and lover is a child molester," Russ said.

"What? A pedophile! No way. What makes you think that?"

"Because he raped me over and over when I was seven. One of the pictures on the wall was of him and the man that kidnapped me and held me for a year, so yeah, he's a pedophile."

Penny's body shuddered. She began crying, sick at the thought of being with him so many times. She got out of the front seat and moved to the back and wrapped her arms around Nickie.

"I'm so sorry, baby. I didn't know."

The three of them sat in the car watching for Rex to reappear with another pile of VHS tapes. He never did.

"Don't move," Russ shouted, as he left the car and ran toward the office. Russ reached the door and saw Rex laying just inside the door, black and red. His flesh burning. His eyes wide. He held more tapes in his arms.

Russ picked up the discarded tapes in the road and began throwing them back in the burning building. The labels, some professionally produced were all child pornography. Russ made sure they burned up with Rex and would never be in circulation again. He grabbed the duffle bag and ran back to the car.

As Russ reached the car, Penny was slipping back into her clothes, and Nickie sat beside her quietly sobbing, resting her head on her shoulder. He threw the duffle bag into the back seat to Penny.

"Tell me if this is what I think it is. If it is, we can give this back to Paul."

Penny unzipped the bag and opened it. It was full of cash. The same rolls and loose cash she took from Turtle's room.

"Yeah, this is one of the bags I took from Turtle's room. It looks like he added some of the cash from the other one into this one," Penny said, as she zipped the bag back up and returned her attention to Nickie.

Russ coughed, spitting up black soot from the back of his throat and spit out the car window. He pulled out of the parking lot and onto the highway as the dark night behind him burned red in his rearview mirror. Gray plumes of smoke rose to the sky. Red embers shot into the air. The car shook from an explosion that sent the contents of the building splintered into the black night.

The darkness in front of them soon erupted into the red and blue lights from the Sherriff's patrol car. He sped toward the bar. As he passed them, he tapped his brakes as if he couldn't make up his mind to go to the bar or turn around and chase them. He finally opted to go check on his friend and source of income. Russ saw the dried dust kick up as Sherriff Tate slid into the parking lot. His lights eventually disappearing behind the flames.

Penny gave Russ directions to her apartment. They sat in the parking lot. Nickie hugged her once more. Russ handed Penny the money she was promised. She refused. He insisted.

"I never thought I would feel so free of him and that place," Penny said. "He was sick. I just didn't know it."

She thanked them both again and got out of the car and walked toward her apartment.

Russ headed toward Highway Fifty-five and pointed the car south.

CHAPTER FIFTY

"Did you talk to him?" Russ asked.

"Yes. He walked me through it, I know what to do," Bubba said. "I'll be right there."

Russ and Bubba arrived at the allotted time. It was early morning. The sleepy town of Lewiston had not yet awakened.

Bubba punched in the code, and they both heard the door click and open slightly. The office was dark and empty since it was Sunday. They were by themselves and would be for as long as they needed.

They walked down a long hallway toward the door at the very end. Two double steel doors opened as Bubba pressed a large round silver plate on the wall. They walked through the doors and into a large white tiled room.

Bubba extracted a folded piece of paper from his front jeans pocket and began reading. He first went to the breaker box and flipped a switch. Lights appeared red on the machine. He pulled a long tray out into the room. Russ placed the suitcase on the tray, and they both pushed it into the chamber. Bubba read from his notes. He flipped a couple more switches and set the temperature dial at eighteen hundred degrees. They smelled gas and soon heard the whoosh of flames. They peered into the window and saw the suitcase catch fire and begin burning.

"Okay. Perry said he would gather the ashes and have them for us tomorrow morning."

"Thanks, Bubba, for everything."

Russ stood and watched as the flames rose higher and higher, completely engulfing the suitcase. As it began to break down, he watched as his father's remains were exposed for the last time and began burning, flames piercing the dark sockets where his eyes once were.

Night

Heavy eyelids pressed down creating darkness. A single spiraling wisp of gray smoke rose.

CHAPTER FIFTY-ONE

Bubba pulled into Russ's driveway just as the blackness of night transformed into the light of day. The boys were all inside still sleeping off the previous night. Fatboy rolled over on the couch as an empty beer can rolled onto the floor from under his increasing girth. Russ laughed at the imprint the beer can made on his stomach, shook his head as he heard him fart, and closed the door behind him.

Russ handed Bubba a coffee through the driver's window as he wound his way around to the passenger side door of Cappy's Bronco. The door squeaked as he opened it and rattled as he closed it. It smelled of burning oil and thirty-three-year-old vinyl seats.

"I'm jealous every time I crawl into this thing," Russ said to Bubba wishing he had taken the Bronco when Cappy offered it to him. He knew how much Bubba loved it and how much Cappy loved Bubba. It was the right thing to do.

They finished eating at Cappy's favorite breakfast place in his honor on the anniversary of his birthday and headed to Beau Chene. They arrived at the maintenance shed, hopped in a cart, and headed toward number ten green.

"The course looks good. Ben's doing a great job," Russ said, marveling at the young golf pro's ability.

Russ cut through two fairways and followed the row of old arthritic oaks toward the number ten green. It was the same route he took the night he killed Randy. As they neared the green, they saw the top of Ben's head disappear behind the green into the sand trap.

"What the hell is he doing out here?" Russ asked, his irritation coming through in his voice.

"Just give him a minute. He's just out here working. He'll leave soon enough," Bubba assured Russ as he patted him on his knee.

Russ and Bubba crawled out of the cart and walked onto the number ten green. They walked to the edge and looked down into the sand trap.

"Ben, what in the hell are you doing out here this early in the morning, son?"

"Oh, hey fellas, I knew you and the boys were starting your tournament today. Just wanted to be sure everything looked good for you, especially number ten," Ben said as he finished raking the sand trap.

Bubba looked at Russ, noticing his reddening face.

"Man, that's really nice of you, Ben. Thanks," Russ said, feeling the humbleness of Ben's actions.

"What are you two doing here this early?"

"Just checking out the crew's work before we got out here. You know we can't have the boys giving us a hard time about our work. You know they'll find something wrong anyway," Russ said as he gave Ben a hand, coming up out of the sand trap.

"All right, I'll leave it with you two. I'm going to check

out the rest of the course," Ben said as he shook each of their hands. "Let me know if you need anything."

"Thanks so much, Ben."

Russ waited for Ben to get out of sight. He walked back over to the cart, and extracted a brown cardboard box. He and Bubba made their way down into the sand trap.

"Do you want to do this by yourself?" Bubba asked.

"I would rather you were here," Russ said, looking at Bubba, both pushing back tears.

Russ opened the box and began spreading Randy's ashes onto the sand trap.

"Why in the hell is this so hard? Why am I so emotional? I hated that son of a bitch."

"I know, but he was still your father. There's a bond there, even if you don't want it to be."

Russ grabbed the rake sitting on the edge of the trap and raked the ashes into the sand.

"Let's go get the boys," Bubba said as he helped Russ out of the trap.

"You don't want to say anything?"

"Nah, nothing left to be said really," Russ said, as he stared down into the sand trap.

Curtis and Fatboy sat in the kitchen, both holding their head in their hands, as Bubba and Russ walked into the kitchen from the garage.

"Where the hell have you two been?" Duckhead asked as he rose from the table with two coffee mugs in his hands.

"Went out to Beau Chene to be sure everything was ready for today and to check on number ten green," Russ said as he stared at Bubba.

"Oh yeah, y'all had to rebuild ten, I forgot about that," Fatboy said around a throaty yawn.

Spanky scampered down the stairs fully dressed, looking for coffee.

"Get dressed, let's go," Spanky said to Fatboy, Duckhead and Curtis.

"What's the rush?" Fatboy asked as he loudly slurped his coffee.

"Man, you look like hell. You should have quit drinking when the rest of us did," Spanky said to Fatboy.

Fatboy said nothing, but thrust his thick middle finger into Spanky's face.

They all finished eating and headed to Beau Chene, where they paired up in carts.

"Hey, let's play together today," Fatboy said to Russ, as they loaded their clubs onto the cart.

They each left the cart shed and in a single file headed over to Cappy's memorial.

"Just like old times, huh, boys?"

"Just like 1982 all over again."

They all arrived at Cappy's marker, stood in a semi-circle, and as usual, tears seeped from their eyes. Memories of a man that loved them all unconditionally filled their minds.

"We're all out here together again, Cap, doing what we love, what you taught us. We're about to go have some fun now, but just know you'll be with us all day like you always are." Fatboy's throat closed as his eyes reddened. He couldn't finish.

"Hey, Cappy wouldn't want to see all of us out here crying like a bunch of girls. We need to raise some hell today and have fun. Let's go play some golf," Bubba said as he quickly ran his finger across his nose.

Happy whoops and hollers sounded from each of the carts as they made their way toward the first hole.

The morning air was crisp and clear. Autumn had finally defeated summer, and the trees around them began to blush, revealing reds, golds, and oranges. The hues of their brilliant annual death before the leaves withered and fell to the ground. The barren gray and gnarled wood of winter would suffer the cold months ahead.

Each of the boys teed off; their drives all landing in roughly the same area. They all finished the first hole as they would the next eight, hovering around par. With the first nine holes complete, they made their way to the nine-teenth hole for a break and early lunch.

They walked in through the kitchen, surprising Ray Ray.

"When did y'all get in town?" Ray Ray asked no one in particular.

"We all got in last night. How have you been man?" Curtis asked, giving Ray Ray a side hug.

"Doin good. Jus' stayin' busy here. Business has been real good since they built that new plant."

"Man, that's great to hear, Ray Ray. Effie would be proud," Russ said, rubbing him on the back.

"What y'all want? Same thing?"

"Yep, six cheeseburgers and some cokes," Russ said speaking for the group.

"Seven," Fatboy said.

"Six," Russ quietly mouthed to Ray Ray holding up six fingers.

The boys finished eating and headed to the number ten tee box. They each took their turns driving, and landed their balls just at the turn of the dogleg. They arrived at their balls, and each played their second shot.

"Damn Bubba, y'all did a great job. This hole looks fantastic," Curtis said as he slid his pitching wedge back into his bag.

Bubba walked over to Russ. "You doing okay, bud?"

"I'm fine."

As they approached the green, three balls were on the green, and two were nowhere to be seen. Curtis and Fatboy checked the balls on the green and soon realized theirs had rolled off into the sand trap.

"Damn, that thing is deep. Shit, that must be ten feet," Fatboy said as he made his way down to his ball.

The rest of the boys stood on the green waiting for Curtis and Fatboy to punch themselves out of the sand. Curtis struck his ball first. The strike was followed by a curtain of sand as his ball bounced just inches away from the hole.

Fatboy stood at his ball and took a couple of practice swings. He screwed his feet into the sand and looked at the top of the flag again. He swung, topped his ball, pushing it deeper into the sand.

Russ watched as another curtain of sand rose and fell onto the green.

Fatboy repositioned himself and struck the ball again. Another thicker curtain of sand pushed the ball up and onto the green, and it landed a foot from the flag.

Curtis stood just outside the sand trap, helped Fatboy out and held onto him, pulling him up to the green.

Russ was furthest away and stood leaning on his club by his ball allowing everyone else to putt. One by one they sunk their putts, finished the hole, and made their way behind Russ. He walked the hole, looking for the break. He noticed the sand that now covered the green and made a point to walk over it, pushing it into the green.

Bubba walked the path as well as if he were Russ's caddy, finding the same break as Russ did. Bubba positioned himself behind the ball and watched as Russ approached his shot and took a couple of short practice putts. His mind was full, filtering the recent events, the bones, the fire, and the ashes.

He struck the ball and it began rolling, following the break just as he and Bubba thought it would. Bubba stood with his arms in the air, celebrating. There was excited chatter from the boys as they watched the ball roll toward the cup. Celebrations flowed from their mouths, and dancing ensued as the ball rolled closer and closer, the intensity growing. The ball rolled within a half-inch of the hole, abruptly turned, and slowly rolled away from the hole, picking up speed as it disappeared into the sand trap.

"Damn, that looks like God himself just blew on that ball, Bubba said.

"That wasn't God, Bubba," Russ said as he walked to the edge of the green and stared down into the trap.

EPILOGUE

Halloween was the first holiday Nickie had celebrated in several years. When she was a little girl Halloween was her favorite holiday. Her mother usually handmade her costumes. It had never been the same in the foster homes. If she had a costume at all it was either a hand-me-down or a cheap paper Walmart classic that was torn up before the end of the night.

The last Halloween Nickie celebrated was when she was sixteen. She spent hours on her costume, sewing, pinning, and adding material here and there; mixing and matching colors and prints. Memories of her mother filled her mind as she sewed fives, tens, and twenties into her coat and pants. The "extra" material she used actually came from the only other clothes she owned. They were patched in and hidden as well as she could hide them. This was the one time that her foster parents' ignoring her actually paid off. They simply didn't see that she was literally wearing every possession she had in the world.

The money she sewed into her clothing had been saved

for months, money from her part-time job. The days she skipped lunch or dinner at work so she could save that much more money were tough, but it worked and prepared her for the hard days ahead.

Before she left, she stole into the kitchen unseen and filled up two bandanas she sewed together to hold as much food as she could fit in them. As she tied the four corners together and onto the cane, her hobo outfit was complete.

She slipped her stepfather's folding knife into her back pocket and headed out the door. The party was held at one of her more-wealthy classmate's home. She spent a few minutes there, quietly saying goodbye to the ones she considered her real friends. There were only a few. It didn't take long. She anxiously walked out of the door and onto the sidewalk that was filled with children in every variety of costume. The children's shrill cries from pure excitement returned her to her childhood, when she walked, holding her mother's hand, along similar sidewalks framed with homes of their well-to-do neighbors. She walked amongst Jack-o-lanterns and stalks of corn leaning on hay bales as they lead her out of the neighborhood and to the nearest railroad tracks. She waited on a train heading anywhere. She waited on a train away from the abuse, away from her current stepfather and his busy hands.

For the next six years she rode trains to every corner of the United States, but those trains eventually lead her back home to Mississippi.

Years later she now stood at the door in another well-to-do neighborhood in her own beautiful home handing out candy. She traded in her hobo outfit, for a new wardrobe handpicked by Jaimey. Her new clothes didn't make her look like a streetwalker, rather they reminded her of how her own mother used to dress.

Jaimey not only helped her with her wardrobe, but made it possible for Nickie to purchase her old childhood home near Beau Chene. She lived right down the street from where Jim and Jaimey lived.

Bubba helped Nickie renovate it and now she stood in her own home, welcoming her guests, and quietly thanking Hugh Jack for making it possible.

She renovated herself as well, working with a therapist on letting go of her anger. Her tattoos and scars from cutting were disappearing along with her improper use of the English language. She was becoming the Southern lady her mother was in the process of raising before she died.

Her new family slowly arrived. Bubba showed up with his girlfriend. Russ and his wife and Will were there. Jaimey and Jim stood at the door, offering food and drinks to everyone.

The night was festive. It was a perfect October evening. A bright harvest moon floated above them. The sky was clear and the air crisp. The leaves on the trees were full into their final moments. Their brilliant golds, oranges, and reds dotting the neighborhood.

As everyone made their way outside to her new deck, laughter filled the air in spurts as the spirits began to flow. Jaimey stood in the middle of the group and asked for the floor. Everyone stared at her in anticipation of her words.

"People usually don't have a story of when they met, like Mad … Nickie and I did. For us to have found each other after all these years is rarely heard of. I … we … all of us, have grown to love her. Family is so important, our family is so important, it's everything,"

Jaimey turned to Nickie and took her hands into hers and stood Nickie up in front of her.

"Nickie, Some of us aren't bound by blood, but we love each other as family."

Jim handed Jaimey an envelope.

"We want you to be a more permanent part of ours," Jaimey said as she handed the envelope to Nickie.

Nickie opened and unfolded the paper. Her eyes moved back and forth with each sentence. They began to redden and fill with tears as she read the last word. She looked at Jaimey, then Jim, and hugged them. Slowly the others joined in, and before long they all stood in a huge blob, hugging and crying.

"Welcome home, sis," Russ said.

"Well?" Jaimey asked as she held a pen in front of Nickie.

Nickie could only manage a nod of her head. She signed the paper and handed it back to Jim.

"Does this mean I get to change my last name to Spencer now?" Nickie asked, as she wiped tears from her face.

The sound of clapping hands echoed in the cool October night, interrupted by the doorbell. Nickie wiped her eyes and moved toward the door. A hobo stood among a small cluster of children. Her bucket was extended toward Nickie on a handle clad in a blue bandana. Nickie dropped in a handful of candy, staring into the bottom as she did. The donuts, crackers, sardines and cheese she had packed all those years earlier stared back at her. Her mind reeled through the first days eating from the bandana. The memory of her tight stomach made her touch her now full belly. She closed the door and turned back toward her family. She scanned the crowd of people who loved each other. She was through running. She was home.